"You have a son."

The space between Shane and Hope vibrated with his shock and something much stronger that came from his gut and surged through his bloodstream.

Hope's hands fluttered. "I had just found out I was pregnant the night I called off the wedding. I couldn't tell you. I didn't want you to marry me for that reason, not when you didn't want children. I couldn't see any other way to go."

Shane could hardly contain his anger. "You could have told me the truth!"

"No, I couldn't, because you would have done the honorable thing despite the way you felt, and that would have been wrong for both of us."

"So you lied," Shane said. "Once you found out you were pregnant, I had a right to know. What's his name?"

"Christopher."

"I want to see him. *Now.*"

Dear Reader;

Silhouette Romance begins the New Year with six heartwarming stories of the enduring power of love. Felicity Burrow thought she would never trust her heart again—until she met Lucas Carver and his darling little boy in *A Father's Vow*, this month's FABULOUS FATHER by favorite author Elizabeth August.

Love comes when least expected in Carolyn Zane's *The Baby Factor,* another irresistible BUNDLES OF JOY. Elaine Lewis was happy to marry Brent Clark— temporarily, of course. It was the one way to keep her unborn baby. What she didn't bet on was falling in love!

Karen Rose Smith's emotional style endures in *Shane's Bride*. Nothing surprised Shane Walker more than when Hope Franklin walked back into his life with a little boy she claimed was his. Loving little Christopher was easy, but trusting Hope again would prove a lot harder. Could Hope manage to regain Shane's trust and, more important, his love?

The sparks fly fast and furiously in Charlotte Moore's *The Maverick Takes a Wife*. When Logan Spurwood fought to clear his name, Marilee Haggerty couldn't resist helping him in his search for the truth. Soon she yearned to help him find strength in her love, as well....

And two couples discover whirlwind romance in Natalie Patrick's *The Marriage Chase* and *His Secret Son* by debut author Betty Jane Sanders.

Happy Reading!

Anne Canadeo

Please address questions and book requests to:
Silhouette Reader Service
U.S.: 3010 Walden Ave., P.O. Box 1325, Buffalo, NY 14269
Canadian: P.O. Box 609, Fort Erie, Ont. L2A 5X3

SHANE'S BRIDE

Karen Rose Smith

Carole,
May the
new year bring
all good things

Karen Rose Smith

Silhouette
ROMANCE™
Published by Silhouette Books
America's Publisher of Contemporary Romance

To Aunt Dawn, my first role model before women *were* role models. I miss you.

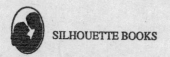

SILHOUETTE BOOKS

ISBN 0-373-19128-6

SHANE'S BRIDE

Printed in U.S.A.

KAREN ROSE SMITH

lives in Hanover, Pennsylvania, with her husband, an elementary school librarian, and their son, a recent college graduate. She has read romance novels since she was a teenager precisely because they end with happily ever after. She thinks everyone needs hope in an ideal and an escape from time to time. And that's why she can see herself reading and writing romance novels for a long time to come.

Shane's Bride is the third romance in her DARLING DADDIES series for Silhouette Romance. Readers can share their views of the heroes in her trilogy—Adam, Jon and Shane—by writing to Karen at P.O. Box 1545, Hanover, PA 17331 and telling her which hero they'd prefer to love!

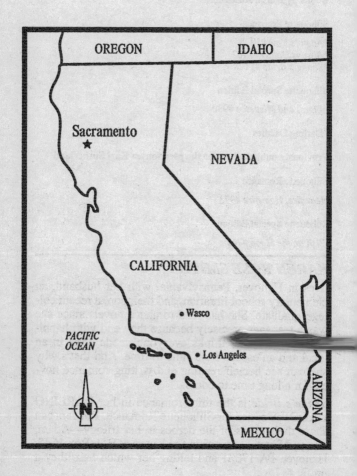

Prologue

Hope Franklin's heart thudded with excitement, but with trepidation too, as she climbed the porch steps to the house where she'd lived all her twenty years. Surely Shane would change his mind once he heard her news. With their wedding only two days away and their future stretching before them, wouldn't he feel joy over a life they'd created together? The child they'd created?

But then she remembered the pain in his voice, on his face, in his hands the night he'd told her about his wife and child and how he'd lost them. His control had snapped and they'd made love that night. The one and only time. He'd needed her and she'd needed him. Afterward, he'd vowed not to make love to her again until their wedding night, until she was protected, until they were truly husband and wife. He was that type of man.

Although she loved children, she had agreed to a childless marriage. She loved Shane so much she would agree to almost anything.

Shane had faced adversity over and over in his life. But instead of making him bitter, it had made him strong, as well as silent, too silent sometimes. During their four months together, she'd worked at drawing him out, letting him know he could tell her anything. And even though he didn't say it often, she knew he loved her. But did he love her enough to accept this child?

Hope had prayed that some day, knowing the love Shane had to give, he would change his mind about their having children. She'd witnessed his work with teenagers at the community center. And he showed her often how much he loved her. She'd pressed fourteen yellow roses between the pages of her books. Every Friday night, he'd brought her one. It signified the completion of another week, their growing feelings for each other and the importance of talking about their successes and failures. Those special times of holding and caring were more precious to her than she could ever explain. The two most recent roses were in a vase on her desk in her bedroom, reminding her daily of the commitment they'd made.

She loved Shane. Still, her fear made her throat tight. What if he couldn't accept this child? What if...

Stopping the questions, she opened the door and went inside. She heard voices coming from the kitchen. Her mother's and Shane's. Quickly she shrugged out of her jacket and hung it in the foyer closet. Flipping her ponytail over her shoulder, she wondered how she could get Shane alone without making her mother too curious. Maybe she could say she wanted to show him the beautiful November sunset. Or maybe she should wait to tell him until after supper. They could drive to Malibu...

"You're a gem, Mrs. Franklin. Your pot roast could win a medal." Shane's tone was teasing but conveyed his appreciation of her mother's culinary talent.

Jennie Franklin laughed. "You can tell from the aroma? I think maybe you just haven't eaten properly all day. And, by the way, Shane, don't you think since you're marrying my daughter this weekend, you could call me Jennie?''

There was a pause. "I'd like that."

Hope understood the huskiness in Shane's voice. He'd lost his own mother and valued the bond he was building with hers.

"Shane, there is something I'd like to discuss with you before Hope arrives."

"Is there a problem?"

Jennie Franklin's tone was gentle. "I don't know. Hope tells me you don't want to have children."

He didn't answer immediately, but finally said, "That's right."

"You know Hope loves children. For three years she's worked in the day-care center. I told her somehow I'd manage to send her to college full-time instead of part-time, but over and over she's reminded me the experience would make her a better teacher when she does get her degree. She loves working with little children. I think she'd do it even if she didn't get paid."

The house was quiet for a few moments as Hope waited for Shane's response.

"We believe our love is enough."

"Your love needs to spill over, Shane. It needs to be bigger than the two of you."

His voice was sad with a raspy catch. "You don't understand."

"Make me understand so I know Hope won't regret this pact she's made with you."

"Did Hope tell you about my wife and son?"

"She told me you're divorced."

"Yes. Because of what happened. Because—"

Hope knew Shane held in his emotions and didn't want to appear vulnerable to anyone. It came from his upbringing, from his years as a member of the police force, from the sticky situations he'd handled as a private investigator, from the loss of his son.

A chair scraped the linoleum and in her mind's eye, Hope could see Shane as he sat in the kitchen chair, his broad shoulders, his short tawny hair, his brown eyes that could hide every thought in his head so well.

"I grew up in the projects."

"Hope did tell me that. I figured it had something to do with you becoming a police officer. But she didn't tell me why you gave it up, why you decided to become a private investigator instead."

"I became a cop because I thought I could clean up the city, make a difference. But it's not possible, Mrs. Franklin." He corrected himself. "Jennie. I was a cop for eight years, and I didn't make a dent, let alone a difference. You wouldn't believe the misery I saw. Then that misery touched me."

"What happened?" she asked softly.

"I was married. We had a six-year-old, Davie, full of life and fun. I was working the night shift, so I was home during the day. One day, Mary Beth and Davie decided to go to the video store for a movie. My car was parked behind hers, and Mary Beth decided to take it to avoid the hassle of getting to her own. Davie ran out ahead of her and opened the driver's door so he could crawl in beside her. The car exploded."

"Oh, Shane."

"I heard Mary Beth's screams. I still hear them. Neither of us could do anything. Later, we found out a guy I'd collared when I was a rookie planted the device as an act of revenge. But the bomb took the wrong person, and I was to blame. Mary Beth blamed me, too. Our marriage fell apart."

"Shane, I'm so sorry."

"I won't bring a child into a world of suffering, into a world that doesn't cherish its children or protect them by keeping criminals like that thug behind bars instead of paroling them. I will never get over losing Davie. Not in this lifetime or the next. Don't you see? I can't have more children. I can't put myself through that again.''

Hope leaned against the closet door. She knew Shane's pain went deep, but she'd hoped their marriage would heal the wounds. Yet, she also knew if he wasn't ready for healing, he'd fight it. A child *could* make the pain deeper instead of healing him. She'd been naive to think the news of her pregnancy might be welcome. Shane said what he believed. He was passionate about what he felt. Could she trap him in a situation he didn't want? What would happen to his feelings for her if she did?

If she told him about the baby, she knew what Shane would do. He'd go through with the wedding because he was an honorable man. But what kind of marriage would they have?

Tears flooded her eyes. Certainly a marriage he didn't want, and a child who would remind him every day of the son he'd lost. He'd resent the pain. He'd resent her. Worst of all, though he'd never admit it, he'd resent their child. She couldn't bear to see the love they'd shared erode with each passing day, each time Shane looked at her and their child and realized he was imprisoned in his anguish.

Her love wasn't strong enough to watch the feelings between them die instead of grow. Yet she had to give them one last chance, one last chance for Shane to put their love before his pain.

With trembling fingers she brushed the tears from her cheeks. Lifting her chin, she walked into the kitchen.

Shane's head came up. His brown eyes warmed just for her. Standing, he took her in his arms and hugged her. ''Hi there.'' His voice was still low and husky from the strain of sharing details of his past with her mother. ''I was worried. Did you get tied up at work?''

''No. I need to talk to you. Let's go into the living room.''

"But your mother has supper ready."

Jennie Franklin's gaze passed quickly over the two of them. "That's all right," she said, sounding worried. "I can keep everything warm."

Shane took Hope's hand and walked with her to the sofa. When they were seated, he wrapped his arm around her and kissed her. Her fear kept her from responding with her usual fervor, and he leaned away, never a man to push or take more than she wanted to give.

The gold in his eyes told her better than words that his desire for her would ignite with a kiss, a touch, a smile. But she had none of them for him now. Meeting his gaze, she took a deep breath. "Shane, I need to ask you something." She unconsciously placed her hand on her stomach. "Do you think you'll ever change your mind about having children?"

The gold disappeared as his eyes darkened with pain. "Hope..."

"I want your children. And I...need to have a baby. To feel fulfilled in our marriage. To feel fulfilled as a woman." A tiny kernel of hope inside her heart urged her to believe that her announcement might change Shane's mind, that they could have a happy future.

The nerve in his jaw worked. "We had an agreement."

A sob lodged in her throat but she pushed out the rest of what she had to say. "I know. But I can't keep it."

For a moment, she saw...devastation. And for that moment, she could see all the pain from the loss of his son that he tried to hide, the depth of the wound she thought she could help heal. She'd been naive again.

Shane turned away, his lean cheeks taut. When he met her gaze again, she couldn't see anything but his dark brown eyes. He'd erected a wall...against her. She could feel it as tangibly as she'd felt his love a second before.

His years of growing up in the projects, his years of sto-
icism as a cop, protected him when he asked, "What are you
trying to tell me?"

Her heart broke and she knew it would never be the same
again. She loved Shane too much to trap him. "That...that
I need to have children and if you truly don't want them,
then I can't marry you."

"Hope..." He spoke her name with such anguish, such
torment. Then all emotion was gone. "You're calling off the
wedding?"

"Shane, I have to. I have to think about the future. Can't
you do that? Can't you imagine—"

He reached for her, then dropped his hand. "No, I can't.
I can't imagine you pregnant, my worrying day after day,
night after night, whether you and the baby will be all right.
I can't imagine caring for an infant, chasing after a toddler,
knowing I can't protect him. And most of all, I can't imagine the ache every time I look at our child because I miss
Davie even more. No, I can't imagine it, Hope, because at
times, even now the pain is unbearable. I can't imagine it
being even worse. If you need children in your life, then
you're right to call off the wedding."

He stood, moving away from her, moving out of her life.
"Tell your mom I won't be staying for dinner. Tell her
whatever you need to tell her."

Hope took one last chance. "Shane, you can't leave like
this. We can talk—"

He shook his head. "There's nothing to talk about. We've
made our choices. Now we'll have to live with them."

His tall body was rigid. She wanted to hold him and make
everything right. But she couldn't. She had to let him go.

Shane Walker didn't meet her gaze again, didn't touch
her, didn't say goodbye. He simply walked out the door.

Chapter One

Four Years Later

In a fog, Hope walked around the house her mother had rented in Los Angeles for most of Hope's life. She picked up a needlework magazine on the coffee table. Crossing to her mother's favorite easy chair, she opened the tapestry bag containing her mother's knitting. A small sweater was almost finished. Jennie Franklin had intended it to be a Christmas present for her grandson. Christmas...a time for families and love and...

Hope had been debating with herself ever since Christopher was born—as she'd fed him, and changed him, and cared for him in Wasco, a small town about two hours away. She'd thought her love for Shane and her memories of him would fade with the years, but they hadn't. She saw Shane in Christopher's brown eyes, the quirk of his smile, the beauty of him. She constantly questioned whether she'd done the right thing when she'd left without telling him about her pregnancy.

With Christopher's first birthday, she'd told herself that Shane had probably gone on with his life. During Christopher's second year, every time she visited her mom, she'd thought about calling Shane. And this past year as Christopher had grown and asked more questions about the world around him, she'd doubted her decision daily.

A month ago, the owners of the day-care facility where Hope worked had informed her they'd be closing at the end of the month. Operating costs were too high and the profit margin not great enough. She had thought about moving back to be with her mother, and she'd sent résumés all over Los Angeles. She'd seriously considered telling Shane they had a son.

Two weeks ago, she had received a phone call in the middle of the night from her aunt, a phone call that changed her life. Her mother's unexpected death had shaken up Hope's world. It had made her look at her life with Christopher more closely—what he needed. They had Aunt Eloise, her mother's sister. But no one else. Christopher needed his father. Soon he'd begin to ask specific questions. Hope couldn't lie to him. She wanted to tell him what a wonderful man his father was. She wanted him to know Shane because he deserved to know his father. Now, all she had to do was pick up the telephone . . .

The doorbell rang and Hope jumped. Maybe it was Aunt El. She'd offered to watch Christopher so Hope could start packing her mother's belongings, so she could spend some time alone with her thoughts in the house where she'd grown up, in the house she'd soon have to vacate.

When she answered the door, a young man in a green uniform stood on the porch. "Eloise Murray told me I could find Hope Franklin here. I have a package for her."

"I'm Hope Franklin."

"Sign here, please."

Hope signed the paper on the clipboard and the man gave her a manila envelope. She thanked him, closed the door and checked the letterhead. It was from her mother's lawyer. Hope had met the white-haired older man when she was a teenager, after her father died.

Slipping her thumb under the flap, she tore open the envelope. Inside, she found a sealed letter along with a note from the lawyer. It read:

Dear Miss Franklin,
Your mother instructed me to deliver this letter to you upon her death. I will call you in a few days to set up a time for the reading of her will.

My sincere condolences,
George Gunthry

With shaking fingers, Hope carefully opened the ivory envelope.

Darling Hope,
I know this will be a difficult time for you. But there is something I'd like you to do. Your father's gold pocket watch is in my jewelry box. I want you to give it to Shane.

George made my will after your father died. I preferred not to tamper with it because I want this bequest to be a personal moment between you and Shane. Before Christopher was born, you made a decision considering Shane's wishes. Maybe it's time to consider yours and Christopher's.

I love you, Hope. All I've ever wanted is your happiness. Be happy, sweetheart, no matter what you decide.

Mom

Was this her mother's way of giving her a last bit of guidance, a gentle shove? Forcing her to confront Shane and her feelings for him?

It was time to face the truth, to let Shane decide if he wanted to be a part of his son's life. It was time to let go of the guilt and the doubts and put the decision in his hands.

On Wednesday afternoon, the heat of a September sun poured onto Hope's shoulders as she rang Shane's doorbell, praying he still worked from an office in his house. Her nervousness increased as she stood on the doorstep of the Spanish-style two-story with its black wrought iron trim and terra-cotta-colored exterior. She'd always loved Shane's house with its old-world charm and cozy interior. Was he sharing it with someone else?

The door opened and a pretty blonde with short hair and a warm smile stood in front of her. Hope was speechless for a moment, though she'd thought about the possibility of Shane's marrying another woman. She swallowed hard, her courage flagging, but her determination took over.

"Hello? Can I help you?" the woman asked as her gaze slid over Hope's yellow dress and bolero jacket.

"I'm looking for Shane Walker. Are you...Mrs. Walker?"

The blonde laughed. "Absolutely not." She extended her hand. "I'm Jana Hobbs, and I work with Shane. Are you trying to find someone?"

"Uh, no. Just Shane."

Jana motioned her to follow. "Come in. He's in the office."

Hope stood in Shane's living room, her emotions tightening her throat. After four long years everything was the same, from the Native American painting above the fireplace to the hand-carved wooden lamps standing like sentinels on either side of the taupe and green tweed sofa. The light-wood end tables, their tops inlaid with mosaic tiles, even held the same bronze sculptures of wild horses Shane had purchased from an art collector. She'd stood beside him as he'd bargained for them. The only new piece of furniture was a chest with bookshelves sitting by the stairway.

Jana motioned to the office, a sun room adjacent to the living room. Hope walked toward it, her heart pounding.

A portable playpen was set up in one corner. But a child wasn't in it. Shane stood by the windows, holding a toddler. Hope couldn't believe it.

Shane said, "I think Matthew's getting another tooth. I have an extra teething ring in the refrigerator—" He turned toward the doorway and went perfectly still.

Hope knew she looked different. The ponytail had gone soon after Christopher was born. Without the weight of its length, her layered chin-length brown hair waved around her face; once pulled back, her bangs now dipped across her forehead. She'd lost some weight, too. Working, and running around after her son, had kept her in shape.

But she wasn't the only one who'd changed. Where Shane had once worn his hair cropped short and neat, it now hung to his shirt collar in the back and over his ears on the sides. As for the rest of him— Her heart tripled its rhythm. In tan slacks and a cream-colored polo shirt, he looked good enough to...hug. But the stance of his body, the expression on his face, told her this wasn't a reunion he'd anticipated or ever expected.

Suddenly, the baby waved his arms and reached for Shane's collar. Shane tore his gaze from Hope's and rubbed the little guy's back as if he'd done it many times before. "I think your mom has plans for you."

Jana laughed. "It's time to go home. He's just trying to coax you into carrying him around a bit longer." She picked up the diaper bag sitting near the playpen, then held out her arms.

Matthew reached for his mother, then swayed back toward Shane with a smile and a gurgle. Shane leaned closer to Jana. "Go on, pal. I'll see you tomorrow."

Jana lifted Matthew from Shane's arms. After a short pout, he snuggled in his mom's arm. "Call me if you have any questions on the notes I made. I'll see you in the morning," she said, glancing at Hope, then back to Shane.

Shane nodded, but his gaze returned to Hope's. It wasn't until the front door closed that he finally looked away.

Hope felt shell-shocked, seeing him again. Memories came rushing back along with old feelings that were still new. She remembered the day she'd met him, the workshop he'd presented at the college, his intensity when he'd talked about guiding teenagers in the right direction instead of letting them end up in the criminal justice system. After the workshop, she'd approached him with a few questions. They'd gone for coffee and talked, becoming more absorbed in each other than in the subject of his presentation. He'd asked her out, and their courtship had begun.

She remembered the kisses, the touches, that one special night. . . .

Hope had matured and changed over the last four years. Watching Shane hold a child in his arms led her to believe he'd changed, too. But her memories and emotions kept her immobilized. Shane had to pass her to get to his desk chair. As he passed, she could have sworn they both held their breaths. The brief contact of his shoulder against hers as he angled around the playpen acted like a jolt of electricity to her already overloaded nervous system.

Not knowing where to start, she said, "Jana said she works with you."

"Yes, she does."

"She brings her baby to work?"

Shane lodged one hip against the desk. "Sometimes."

"How old is . . . it's Matthew, isn't it?"

"Fifteen months." The lines along Shane's mouth that carved into his lean cheeks when he smiled now looked deeper than they had four years ago.

Hope couldn't keep the burning question in her mind. "Is Matthew yours?"

Shane looked as though he might not answer, but then in a brisk tone explained, "Jana is happily married to a friend of mine. Matthew is theirs."

"I was surprised to see you with a child."

"I never said I didn't like kids. I just didn't want to bring any into the world."

When the silence stretched into an unbearable awkwardness, he asked, "Why are you here?"

There was no welcome in his voice, none of the gentleness she knew he was capable of conveying. The wall he'd erected the last time they'd talked, the day he'd left her mother's house, was solid and sturdy. All she could do was take one step at a time.

"My mother passed away two weeks ago." Hope's throat tightened and she had to fight back the tears that were all too quick to come to the surface these days.

Shane's stony expression softened. "I'm sorry. I know how much she meant to you."

Yes, he did. In fact, he'd known everything about her because she'd held nothing back. Not until she'd received the news of her pregnancy. "I've been staying at Aunt El's."

"How's your aunt taking this?" he asked, his tone bringing back memories of his arms around her, confidences shared, yellow roses.

She shook off the images, and the feelings that went with them, to concentrate on his question. Her aunt Eloise and her mother had been close all their lives. "It's difficult for her."

Shane stuffed his hands into his pockets, a familiar gesture. He always did it when he was uncomfortable. "I'm sorry about your mother, but you could have sent me a note. Why did you come?'' He seemed genuinely perplexed.

''Because Mom left me a letter. She wants you to have something of my dad's.''

The seconds ticked by. ''Why?''

''She . . . she just wanted you to have it. Because she liked you, Shane.'' Hope knew Shane's memories of his mother weren't all happy ones, that's why she'd hoped he could share her mother. It was too late. But it wasn't too late for him to have a relationship with his son. ''I wanted to invite you over to Mom's house to pick it up. How about tomorrow sometime?''

Shane looked torn. Finally, he said, ''All right. Around one?''

''That's fine. I'll look forward to seeing you then.''

Shane pushed away from his desk. ''I'll walk you out.''

He didn't try to make conversation as he walked Hope to the door. He felt numb. He'd never expected to see Hope Franklin again. He'd told himself she was history. But he couldn't look at a yellow rose, couldn't look at the tux still hanging in his closet, couldn't close his eyes sometimes, without wondering what they could have had, without wondering why he still missed her and wondering if she was now married to someone else, mothering the children she'd wanted.

The sense of betrayal he'd experienced when she'd called off the wedding had never ebbed. He'd fallen in love with her and he'd trusted her—with his heart, with his life. But he hadn't been enough for her. His love hadn't been enough. She'd wanted more. She'd wanted something he couldn't give her, because in giving her a child, he would have given himself unending heartache. In four years, his grief over his dead son hadn't lessened, it had taken a deeper foothold. Hope's broken promise had made him more guarded, and he knew he'd built an impenetrable shell around his heart.

So why did Hope's presence in his house make that shell feel not quite as secure, as if it needed another fortifying layer?

Shane glanced at her again. If he looked too hard, too long, he might feel something after she left that could only hurt him more. She was so damn pretty. Those big blue eyes once filled with optimism and sparkling enthusiasm now reflected sadness and something else he couldn't put his finger on. But it didn't matter. After tomorrow, he'd never see her again.

He opened the door for her. When she stepped over the threshold onto the porch, he called, "Hope?"

She turned.

"Don't go to any trouble tomorrow. I won't be able to stay. I have appointments later in the afternoon."

As soon as he saw her disappointment, he regretted his abrupt words. She looked as if she was about to say something, but then changed her mind. Instead, she nodded. "I'll see you tomorrow around one."

Shane watched her walk down the path to her car, wishing he could deny her effect on him, wishing tomorrow was over so feelings he'd kept in check for four years could stay buried.

Shane walked up the steps to Jennie Franklin's house, remembering the last time he'd left it, the night Hope had called off the wedding.

He'd thought he was over her. He'd thought he'd gone on with his life. But just one look at her, the scent of her, the lift of her eyebrow when she was unsure, was enough to make every nerve in his body need. And not for just any woman, but for her. He hadn't slept last night. Not that insomnia was new to him. But too many memories had come crashing back.

When he rang the doorbell, Hope answered immediately. She must have been waiting. She was dressed in a navy jumpsuit that wasn't intentionally seductive, but hinted at her curves. The hint was enough. He'd always loved her long hair, but he had to admit the shorter style framed her face in a way that made him want to touch it, to brush her cheek, to... He gave himself a mental kick.

"Come in," she said softly.

That damn soft voice. He'd never heard it raised in anger. "I can't stay long." He knew he was curt, but he had to watch every response, every syllable, every thought.

She led him to the living room couch. He chose a side chair. Not commenting, she lifted a small felt pouch from the coffee table. "This is what Mom wanted you to have."

Her fingers brushed his palm and the years slipped away. Heat forked through him and he remembered the night they'd made love. He would never forget that night as long as he lived—the intimacy, the closeness, the sheer pleasure. Focusing on the pouch, he opened it and shook the contents into his hand. A gold watch. Her father's watch. A lump formed in Shane's throat.

"Hope, I don't know what to say."

"You don't have to say anything. I think Mom had a reason for giving that to you."

He heard the seriousness in her voice and his investigative senses went on alert. More was going on here than a bequest. Hope had come back into his life for some reason. "Why did she give it to me?"

He watched Hope's breasts rise and fall as she took a deep breath. "I've been living in Wasco, Shane. When Mom died, I wasn't with her. It was a heart attack, out of the blue...." Her words faded and she blinked away emotion.

He wanted to comfort her, but he knew better and stayed put. "Hope?"

She regained her composure. "When Mom died, I had to rethink decisions I'd made. Decisions that involved you."

He cocked his head and listened intently, to hear what she *wasn't* saying. "Go on."

"At the time, I felt it was best. I thought— Well, it doesn't matter what I thought. The last four years I've been doubting my decision. Since Mom died, I realized I was wrong and you need to know."

"What do I need to know?" he asked slowly, expecting a shock, trying to prepare himself for whatever was coming.

"You have a son. I had just found out I was pregnant the night I called off the wedding."

The buzz of a lawn mower penetrated the windows. The space between Shane and Hope rippled with his shock and something much stronger that came from his gut and surged through his bloodstream.

Hope's hands fluttered. "I couldn't tell you. I didn't want you to marry me for that reason, not when you didn't want children. I couldn't see any other way to go."

He could hardly contain his anger, his sense of betrayal. He felt like a volcano ready to erupt. "You could have told me the truth!"

"No, I couldn't have. Because you would have done the honorable thing despite the way you felt, and that would have been wrong for both of us."

He'd never imagined Hope could lie or deceive. He'd trusted her and this was how she'd repaid that trust. Fury rushed through him, vibrating in his quick response. "So you did the dishonorable thing. You lied," he added, his voice sharp and meant to cut through her.

"I didn't lie. I told you I wanted children. I wanted this baby. I never could have given him up for adoption or—"

Shane leaned forward, his arms braced on his knees, his breathing fast, his heart pounding. "Don't say it. I can't believe *you* believed I'd want you to do either. Not after what we shared." He remembered her telling him she loved him. He remembered loving her.

Her voice shook. "You didn't want children!"

He straightened and tried to rein in his reaction so he could think clearly, so he could get the information he needed. "No, I didn't. But once you found out you were pregnant, I had a right to know. What's his name?"

"Christopher," she said quietly.

Pictures of Davie flashed in Shane's mind. Every one of them hurt to see. "Where is he?"

"Right now he's with Aunt Eloise, at her house."

"I want to see him. *Now*." He was prepared for any argument she might give to keep him away from his son.

"All right. I would have brought him with me but I didn't know if you'd want to think about this—"

"There's nothing to think about." He stood. "Let's go. I remember where your aunt lives. I'll follow you." He wouldn't let Hope out of his sight until he saw his son. And then ... One step at a time.

Hope locked the door, and they went to their cars. She wished she could say something to cut the tension between them, to diffuse Shane's anger, but she realized she had to let it wear off. She had to be patient. And she would be patient for as long as it took. Because she still loved this man.

She always would.

When she pulled into the driveway of her aunt's house, she took a few deep breaths. She had no idea what Shane's reaction would be when he saw his son, but she'd soon find out. She didn't wait for Shane but went to the door, opened it and called to her aunt. "I'm back."

"We're in the kitchen," her aunt responded. "Cookie time."

Shane's car screeched to a stop in front of the house. He ran up to the porch and came in behind her.

"Christopher's in the kitchen with Aunt El."

Shane grasped Hope's arm. "Does he know?"

"What?"

"Will he know I'm his father?"

"No. I haven't talked to him about it yet because I wasn't sure what you'd want to do."

He released her, but the heat from his skin remained. "Introduce me as his father. That's what I am, that's what I'll always be."

Lord, she wished she had a child psychologist at her elbow. She supposed the best thing to do was to be honest with her son in the simplest way possible. "Give me a few minutes to explain to him."

Shane searched her face, his eyes probing, the anger still in evidence. "All right. That's probably best for him. I'll wait here."

Hope breathed a sigh of relief and went to the kitchen.

Her aunt Eloise stood at the counter mixing a meat loaf. "I saw Shane get out of his car."

"As soon as I told him, he insisted on coming over."

Eloise smiled. "Good."

Christopher was eating a cookie. Hope crossed to him and sat beside him. "Hi, honey. How was your morning?"

He took another bite of the cookie. "Okay."

"I need to talk to you about something."

Christopher kept munching.

"Remember when you asked me if you had a daddy, I said you did but he lived somewhere else?"

Her son nodded.

"What would you think about meeting your dad?"

Christopher's eyes brightened and he smiled. "A daddy like Patti's?"

Patti was one of Christopher's friends from day-care. Her father picked her up every day. "He's *your* dad so he wouldn't be exactly like Patti's. He's is the living room. Should I get him?"

Christopher nodded and put the cookie on the table.

Hope returned to the living room and saw Shane pacing. "He's looking forward to meeting you." It sounded so formal. But what else could she say? She didn't know what was going to happen any more than Shane did as he followed her to the kitchen.

"Hello, Shane," Eloise said simply. Her aunt had invited her and Shane to dinner a few times when they were engaged.

Shane nodded then asked, "Did you know?"

Eloise looked fondly at Christopher, then regretfully at Shane. "Yes, I did."

Shane frowned, and Hope went over to her three-year-old. "Honey, this is your daddy."

Her son looked up at her with wide brown eyes. Hope swallowed hard. "Shane, this is Christopher."

Shane approached slowly, as if he couldn't believe the three-year-old in front of his eyes. The lines deepened around his mouth and his quick intake of breath told her he was remembering another little boy, another son. The pain on his face was almost more than she could stand. Would seeing Christopher always bring him pain? How would that pain affect his relationship with Christopher, with her?

Shane crouched beside his son and glanced at the pile of crumbs in front of him. "I guess you like chocolate chip cookies."

"Mommy's an' Auntie El's."

"I know your mommy makes a great chocolate chip cookie. How many have you had?"

Christopher looked up at Hope then leaned closer to Shane and held up three fingers. "I ate two."

Shane smiled.

Christopher took a cookie from the plate in the middle of the table and offered it to Shane. "Want one?"

Shane's smile faded as he took the cookie and stood, leaning against the table as he munched on it. From experience, Hope knew he was reining in emotions, thinking, letting logic decide his next step. He said to his son, "Maybe you and I could go outside and take a walk in the backyard. What do you think?"

Christopher looked up at Hope. Trying to protect her son but wanting to give Shane every opening she could, she asked Christopher, "Do you want to?"

Her son examined Shane's six-one stature, from his face to his sneakers. "Okay." Checking with his mother again, he asked, "Is he a stranger?"

Hope glanced at Shane—the curling light brown hair at the gap in his shirt where two buttons stood open, his taut stomach, his long legs and tanned arms, and she took another deep breath. "No, he's not a stranger." She and her son had talked many times about not playing or speaking with people he didn't know unless she was there. Daddy or not, he didn't know Shane.

Shane's gaze met hers briefly. She felt the shock of it to her toes, anger mixed with anguish and accusation. Taking a towel from the handle of the oven, she wiped her son's mouth and hands, then brushed her hand across his fine, silky hair the same shade as hers. "Maybe you can show your daddy the pretty rocks you found."

Christopher jumped from his chair and went to the door. "See rocks?"

Shane followed his son. "Sure."

Christopher chattered about where he'd found his treasures, his voice fading as they walked down the yard.

Eloise put her arm around her niece's shoulders. "It'll work out, dear. You'll see."

"He's angry with me, Aunt El."

Her aunt patted her shoulder. "Of course he is. He has a right to be."

Hope thought about it as she had a million times before. "I couldn't marry him. It would have been wrong. But I should have stood my ground, *not* married him, and then told him about the baby."

Eloise dropped her arm and went to peer out the door at Shane and her great-nephew. "You were young, Hope. Shane was ten years older than you and a strong-minded man. If he'd insisted on marriage, I'm not sure you could have held out against him."

To see Christopher walk beside Shane gave Hope great joy. To watch Shane take his son's hand also caused her great sadness because she'd kept them apart. How could she ever make up for that? Her aunt's words penetrated. Could she have held out against Shane if he'd wanted marriage back then? "I don't know. Maybe that's why I did it the way I did. But I do know I'm going to move back here and give Shane as much time as he wants with Christopher. I owe him that."

"You don't know what kind of father he'll be."

"I think I do. Just look at them."

Father and son hunkered down over a pile of rocks. Christopher pointed out something.

"The novelty might wear off."

Hope knew her aunt was playing devil's advocate. "No. Shane's not that type of man. He doesn't pretend what he doesn't feel."

Eloise faced her niece. "Do you think he'll be staying for supper?"

"I have no idea, Aunt El. I have no idea what Shane's going to do. I'll have to wait and see."

Sitting in the sun on the warm grass beside Christopher, Shane couldn't help staring at the boy. He looked so much like Davie. His features—Davie's features. His eyes—Davie's eyes. Had Christopher looked like Davie as an infant, as a one-year-old? How old was he when he cut his first tooth, said his first word, took his first step?

Shane still couldn't believe Hope had lied to him, couldn't believe she'd left him and cheated him out of three years with his son. Finding it hard to absorb, fighting off the dark anger he didn't want to influence his attitude toward Christopher, he suddenly felt the immensity of the responsibility that had fallen on him from out of nowhere. Without warning, or time to prepare, he was a father again. This time, he had to do it right. This time he had to make sure his son was safe every minute of every day. He didn't want to let the boy out of his sight. Yet he knew he had to temper his fears.

What was Hope planning? Why had she told him now? Was she willing to move back to L.A.? Would she let him be a parent?

She had no choice. No matter where she lived, Christopher was Shane's son and he'd get to know his child one way or another. The problem was—how was he going to handle having Hope back in his life?

The way he handled everything else. Very carefully.

"Look, Daddy."

The sound of the title, the childlike quality of Christopher's voice, tore Shane apart. Because he remembered another time, another voice. Yet when Christopher handed him the gray stone and his small fingers touched Shane's palm, Shane felt the pride of fatherhood again. Yes, this time he would do it right.

A half hour later, when Shane and his son returned to the kitchen, Christopher ran to his mother. "Milk, Mommy? Daddy drinks milk, too!"

Hope's gaze met Shane's with uncertainty. The fact of the matter was, he felt such confusion about Hope right now, he knew he needed time away from her and Christopher to think, and plan, and decide the best route to take. He certainly didn't trust her. He might never be able to trust her again.

Hope went to the refrigerator and opened the door, pulling out the milk carton. "Shane, would you like to stay for a while, maybe for dinner?"

Shane looked at Christopher and then back at her. "No. I have to get back. I left some work unfinished." He turned to his son. "But I'll see you again. Soon." He ruffled

Christopher's brown hair. "We can have milk and cookies together next time. Okay?"

Christopher bobbed his head enthusiastically.

Hope waited for the three-year-old to sit at the table, then she poured him a glass of milk. "I'll be right at the front door. Aunt El's in her sewing room. If you go in there with her, don't touch anything unless she says you can."

Shane had trouble tearing himself away from Christopher, putting physical distance between them. After a last long look, he walked to the front door. Hope stood a few feet from him.

His voice was gruff with all the unsaid thoughts and feelings churning inside him. "Are you going back to Wasco?"

She straightened her shoulders and tilted up her chin, looking directly into his eyes. "What do *you* want, Shane?"

The question she should have asked four years ago intensified the churning, and he couldn't keep the anger at bay. "So now you're going to think about that?"

"I've always thought about what you wanted and didn't want."

She was lying. She couldn't have thought about him and still kept Christopher away for so long. Silence stretched between them until he said in a low tone, "I need time to think. Just don't go running off without telling me. Because if you do—"

She didn't let him finish his warning. "I won't. Do you want to spend time with Christopher tomorrow?"

Could he believe she wouldn't run? Could he believe she'd stay at least until they made some decisions? He looked into the kitchen where his son was still drinking his milk. "I'll call you."

And with that, Shane stepped onto the porch and closed the door behind him, in more turmoil than he'd experienced in years.

Chapter Two

Shane walked into his office, expecting to be alone. But Jana was still there, sitting at her desk, sorting through mail. "You missed your appointment with Mrs. Johnson. I took down the information and told her you'd call her."

"Damn! I forgot."

"You don't forget appointments, Shane. What's going on?"

Shane walked over to Jana's son who was sleeping peacefully in the portable playpen. He couldn't begin to sort out his feelings for himself, let alone tell Jana about them. In his mind he saw Christopher as he'd sat playing in the sun. Pain sliced through him again.

"Shane? What's wrong?" Jana's voice was worried.

Though Jana had psychic powers that helped her find missing persons, she used her intuition more than she used her "gift" to tune in to people. That's why their partnership as private investigators worked so well. Her intuition matched with his skill, logic and contacts could find almost anybody. That's what he did now—he found people. He didn't get in the middle of divorces or track down thieves anymore.

Jana was waiting for an answer, and he knew she wouldn't let him evade her. Of course, that was the downside of their partnership, sometimes she was too intuitive. "Hope and I . . . have a history."

"This room sizzled yesterday with whatever is between the two of you."

Shane went to the window and stared outside. "Four years ago, she walked out on our wedding because I didn't want kids. Today, she told me we have one. He's three plus a few months and his name is Christopher." Shane had told few people about his background, but Jana and her husband, Adam, knew about his childhood, as well as about Mary Beth and Davie. He'd never told them about Hope.

"What are you going to do?"

He ran his hand through his hair. "That's the million-dollar question. I just met him. He's great. Intelligent, friendly, curious . . ."

"His mother probably had a lot to do with that."

Shane scowled. "Maybe. But every time I look at him . . ." He swore. "This is why I didn't want more kids. How can I protect him, keep him safe, give him everything he needs—"

"How does Hope feel about you spending time with him?"

Shane tried to shove away the anger and the ache in his heart whenever he pictured Hope so he could think more clearly. Sinking into his desk chair, he wheeled to face Jana. "You know, you ask a lot of questions."

Jana put down the letters. "You know, I care."

He could be himself with Jana and her husband. And they did care about him. "I haven't thought about all the questions, let alone the answers. How would you feel if you were just told you had a son and you'd missed the first three years of his life?"

"Angry. Rattled. Confused."

Shane rocked back and forth on the springs of his chair. "Yeah. All three. Plus. Except I know one thing. I'm not going to lose him like I lost Davie. I just have to figure out the best way to deal with all this."

"What about his mother?"

Shane stopped rocking. "What about her?"

"What do you feel?"

He stood and paced the office. "Angry! She ran out on me. She lied to me. And yet, when I look at her..." He stopped pacing and more to himself than to Jana, he muttered, "I still get turned inside out."

"You don't have to take on the problems of the world by yourself, you know. Adam and I are here if you want to talk."

"That's not my style."

"You might have to change your style to handle this one."

Shane's mind buzzed with scrambled pictures from the past—Mary Beth and Davie, the first day he'd met Hope on the college campus where he was giving a seminar on teenagers and the criminal justice system, the day she'd agreed to marry him, the night she'd called it off. All of it still hurt. Too damn much. There was no way he could begin to talk about it, not even with Jana and Adam.

And Hope... No matter what happened with Christopher, he would protect himself this time. He wouldn't let her in. He wouldn't give her the chance to hurt him again.

Hope cut sandwiches into halves, then stacked them on a plate. When she glanced up at the kitchen clock, her heart beat faster. Shane would be stopping by soon. Usually they finished lunch by the time he arrived to play with Christopher, but she'd spent the morning at her mother's trying to pack up the dining room, so they hadn't eaten yet.

Every day for a week, Shane had visited his son, playing with him, building with blocks, digging in the soil, making mud pies. He tried hard to hide his thoughts, but Hope could see the strain on his face, in his body language. She knew he was remembering Davie; she knew he resented her. But instead of putting it into words, he was keeping it inside. She wanted to help him, but he wouldn't let her get close. Their conversations were superficial, the tension between them always simmering. She kept telling herself that she was prepared for his anger, but part of her kept hoping he'd understand and forgive her.

Expecting him, she'd left the front door open. When Shane rang the bell, she called, "Come in."

He entered the kitchen, his jeans, T-shirt and longish hair enhancing his rugged male appeal. "You shouldn't let just anybody wander in."

"I knew you'd be coming."

"This isn't Wasco, Hope."

She sighed. "I know that. I grew up here, remember?" One look into his eyes told her he remembered other things, too. "I'm sorry Christopher's not ready. We didn't have lunch yet. We were over at Mom's, packing up."

"How's it going?"

"Slowly. It's hard."

"I could have come by this evening, instead."

"No, this is fine. It's difficult for me to be there very long."

"Is there anything I can do to help?"

She stopped arranging the sandwich halves and faced him. She could see by the expression on his face that he wasn't offering out of politeness. Maybe he did have some feelings left for her. If he did, they could build on those. "Not at this stage. I have to do a lot of sorting. I did want to ask you if you could possibly come a little later tomorrow and watch Christopher for me."

Her heart beat faster as he came to the counter where she was standing.

"Do you and Eloise want to spend the afternoon at your mom's?"

"No. Aunt El and I have to go to the reading of Mom's will. It shouldn't take long, an hour, if that. I can take Christopher along, but if you'd like to spend time with him, I can ask him if he wants to stay with you."

Shane stared at the plate of sandwiches for a moment, then looked at her. "Is that what you want? Or would you like me to come along?"

"You'd do that?"

Shane shrugged. "I'm Christopher's father. There might be good reason for me to sit in."

She should have known he wouldn't go just to give her moral support. "Of course, I should have thought of that. Christopher can take his coloring book. That should occupy him. My appointment is at two."

"Two should be fine. Jana will be in the office tomorrow."

Now that they were talking, she had to tell him about her plans. "I wanted to tell you—I'll be moving back to L.A. I've sent résumés to every day-care center in the area."

"What about your life in Wasco? Can you leave it that easily?"

She thought he looked relieved about her decision, but it was hard to tell. "About a month ago, I'd decided to look for a job in L.A. The day-care center where I worked closed and I had to make a change, anyway. I was trying to get up the courage to tell you about Christopher when Mom died."

Shane shifted against the counter and his arm brushed hers. "So I'll be able to see Christopher whenever I want."

It wasn't a question, but a challenge. "You can see him whenever you want... *within reason.*"

He looked as if he hadn't expected her to stand up to him. But she wouldn't let her guilt override what was best for their son.

"And who's going to decide what's within reason?" he asked blandly, though his eyes had darkened.

"We'll have to compromise or let Aunt Eloise be the judge. She'd be fair."

He was standing so close that she could see the blond hairs mixed with light brown on his forearms, smell his after-shave, trace his shoulder muscles in the worn T-shirt. For a moment, she thought she saw respect in his eyes, if nothing else, and in that same moment, she thought he leaned closer.

Then, like a crack of thunder startling her, the back door opened and Christopher scrambled in. "Is lunch ready?"

Shane stepped away, his expression unreadable. Hope felt shut out again and was left with an emptiness she'd known for far too long.

After reading Jennifer Franklin's will, George Gunthry laid the document on the blotter in front of him and summed it up, "In essence, Jennie's personal effects as well as the proceeds of the sale of the property in Arizona go to Hope. Do any of you have any questions?"

Shane shifted in the straight-back chair beside Hope's.

On Hope's other side, her aunt asked, "So what do you suggest we do first, Mr. Gunthry? How long does my niece have before she has to vacate the house?"

The white-haired lawyer responded kindly, "Spend some time in the house sorting through Jennie's things. Decide what you'd like to keep. I suggest we call an auctioneer for the rest. Because Jennie rented from Mr. Hale for so long, he's giving you until the end of October to vacate."

Hope tightened her hand around her purse. "It will be difficult auctioning off the furniture I've seen my mother use all her life."

"Would you rather keep it?" the lawyer asked.

"I have to find a job and rent a place for us. I don't know if I can do that in a month."

Her aunt asked the lawyer, "What if she'd rent her mother's house?"

Hope shook her head. "It's too big. We don't need that much room. Besides, I can't rent anything until I find a job."

Shane shifted again and asked, "How soon would you have to set up the auction?"

"That depends on Hope," Gunthry responded.

"I'll need a week or two to decide...." Hope's voice trailed off as she thought about it.

"I'm afraid that's all the time you have, Hope, unless you want to put the furniture in storage. Let me know by October first, all right? That way we can set up the auction and advertise it."

Christopher, who was sitting at Hope's feet with his coloring book, tugged at her hand. "Look, Mommy."

She smiled at her son. "That's nice, honey."

He tugged at her hand again. "Mommy..."

Shane crooked his finger at the little boy. "Come here and show me. Your mom's trying to talk to Mr. Gunthry."

Both Hope's and Christopher's heads swung toward Shane. It seemed strange having someone else directing her son. But if Christopher was going to see Shane as his father, she had to back him. "Show your dad and I'll look at the pictures later."

Christopher's lip sagged in a pout until Shane held out his arms, then Christopher crawled onto his father's lap and pointed to the picture he'd just colored. The two of them were definitely forming a bond.

Hope realized she had to get on with her life, not look toward the past. "I'll make up my mind soon. You'll take care of the property in Arizona?"

"I'll research the real estate companies in the area and find the most competent one. But it could take a while to sell it with the market the way it is. From what I understand, it's in a remote area." He paused. "Do you have any other questions?"

"Not now," Hope answered. "Whatever we get for the Arizona property, I'd like to set aside for Christopher for college."

"We can discuss that when it sells," the lawyer suggested.

While Eloise asked the attorney a question about inheritance tax, Shane leaned toward Hope, his arm brushing hers. "What is the property in Arizona?"

"Just a plot of land Mom and Dad bought for their retirement." Her throat tightened. This appointment had been difficult for her. The reading of the will made everything seem more final. She'd lost both of her parents and hanging on to their possessions wouldn't help. She'd just have to hold on to them with her heart. If she only had a short time to make decisions, she'd better get busy.

"Shane, would it be all right if you saw Christopher tomorrow evening? I'm going to spend the day at Mom's."

He searched her face, then nodded. "No problem."

Where their son was concerned, they didn't have a problem. At least not yet. But from Shane's pensive expression, she wondered if they might not have one soon.

The next afternoon, Hope laid her mother's clothes in piles, sorting the casual everyday slacks and tops from the dresses her mother had worn to church. Eloise had insisted Hope go through her mother's personal effects herself while she worked in the kitchen and kept Christopher occupied.

Hope was buttoning a blazer when she heard footsteps on the stairs and knew instantly they were Shane's. Why was he here? After the reading of the will, he'd been quiet. He'd given Christopher a hug outside the lawyer's office and told Hope he'd see her this evening.

Shane came into the bedroom, wearing navy shorts, a red polo shirt and sneakers that made him look more like a tennis coach than a P.I. Although Hope could feel his gaze on her, she positioned the blazer on top of the other clothes and returned to the closet, removing a handful of dresses.

"How's it going?" he asked gently.

"Fine."

"Christopher looked as busy as your aunt. He's helping her empty the kitchen cabinets."

Hope could still see her mother cooking in that kitchen, still almost smell the pumpkin bread and apple pie that were her specialties. She spoke past the lump in her throat. "Helping?"

Shane chuckled. "He was using two lids as cymbals."

Hope put one of her mother's dresses on the pile on the bed. "Maybe I should bring him up here for a while and give Aunt El a break."

"Maybe *you* should take a break. Eloise said you've been at this since nine o'clock this morning. It's almost two."

"I took a break for lunch." She gazed at a green-and-white print dress that had been one of her mother's favorites.

Shane crossed to the middle of the room where three cardboard boxes stood, one with pocketbooks, one with hats, one with odds and ends. "Hope, you don't have to do this all in one day."

"It won't get any easier. I just have to do it." She laid the green-and-white dress with the others. "Did you need something? I mean, since you came over?"

"No. I thought I would take Christopher to the playground so you and your aunt can work uninterrupted."

Shane's unexpected appearance and kindness was more than Hope could handle at that moment. The ice blue suit of her mother's she held in her hand had been special. She'd helped her mother pick it out. Jennie Franklin had worn it for her twentieth wedding anniversary the year before she'd lost her husband.

Suddenly, the immensity of Hope's loss shook her. She couldn't keep her chin from quivering as her eyes filled with tears. This time she couldn't stop them. Turning toward the closet, she hoped Shane wouldn't see.

"Do you think Christopher will go with me without you?" he asked.

All she could do was nod as she tried to swallow a sob.

"Hope?"

"I'm sure he'll—"

The hand on her shoulder stopped her pretense. Shane nudged her around and saw the tears coursing down her cheeks. "What's wrong?" he asked so gently her tears flowed freer.

"I miss Mom so much. And Dad. It's like I've lost him all over again. I can't believe they're both gone." Her shoulders shook, and she bowed her head.

Blessedly, she felt Shane's arms around her, and she sobbed into his chest. He held her close, and she cried as she hadn't been able to since being notified of her mother's death.

Shane didn't say anything. Hope was thankful because there was nothing anyone could say. The loss was too fresh, the pain too sharp for words to comfort. But the warmth of Shane's body against hers and the strength of his arms did comfort. They stood that way a long time, her cheek and hands pressed to his chest. The feel and smell of him were familiar, awakening more than comfort, reminding her of the night they'd shared.

The beat of his heart, strong and rhythmic, hastened under her hand. His heat surrounded her, becoming steamier the longer they stood together. His muscles grew taut, and she could feel tension spread through him.

He pulled away and she felt cold and alone...alone enough to look up at him with the longing she felt. His jaw tightened, and he took another step back. She saw his chest rise and fall as he pulled a long draft of air into his lungs.

The next instant, his expression was set, control and restraint evident in the straightness of his shoulders, the rigidity of his stance.

The same control made his voice even. "I'll send Christopher up so you can talk to him about going with me."

Just as quickly as Shane had entered the room, he disappeared.

Hope pulled in a few deep breaths of her own. Taking a tissue from the box on the dresser, she blew her nose. The tension between her and Shane was getting worse instead of better, and she didn't know what to begin to do about it.

Three weeks had passed. Hope pushed a carton aside with her foot as she readied her mother's belongings for public auction. Just last week, she'd gone to two preliminary job interviews. But she hadn't heard anything yet. She had some savings, but not enough to put her mother's furniture in storage. So she'd had no choice but to go ahead with the auction. Without a job, she couldn't rent an apartment. Eloise was insisting she and Christopher stay with her as long as they needed to. But Hope had always been independent. She'd raised Christopher on her own, and she wanted them to be on their own now. But until she found a job, that wasn't possible.

Many days during the past three weeks, Shane had come to entertain Christopher so Eloise and Hope could work at Jennie's house without distraction. Hope had thanked him often, but he didn't seem to want her thanks. He didn't seem to want anything from her except time with their son.

She'd gone back to Wasco, packed up her apartment and left the boxes she couldn't fit into her car with the apartment manager. She'd taken Christopher along and Shane hadn't protested. He seemed to think about what was best for Christopher as much as she did. He'd realized Christopher needed to say goodbye to Wasco, too.

Today, the day before the auction, Shane had offered to help with the heavy work. Between watching Christopher and dealing with memories associated with her mother's possessions, Hope hadn't had time to think about herself and Shane... at least not this morning.

She opened the upstairs hall closet. It seemed empty, but she knew she should check the back of the top shelf. She found a step stool in one of the bedrooms and climbed up. A large shoebox zigzagged across the back corner. Leaning forward, she tried to catch the lip with her finger. She'd managed to snag it when the step stool tilted. The next thing she knew, the box had spilled over the shelf, and Shane had swept her into his arms.

Her heart raced and her throat went dry. He'd discarded the cotton shirt he'd worn with his jeans. The muscle shirt he'd worn underneath left nothing to her imagination—not his muscles, not his tanned skin, not the springy hair tickling her arm.

"You should be more careful." His husky voice fell over her, and although it was October, she felt as hot as she would in August.

"I will be," she squeaked, aware of the rise and fall of his chest, his heart speeding with hers. Clearing her throat, she tried again, "I'll put the phone book on the stool."

He arched his eyebrows and grimaced. "Oh, that's real careful," he drawled as he set her on her feet.

"I have to finish emptying everything."

"So call if you need help."

"I don't want to take advantage of your help."

Shane's brown eyes held her for an interminably long moment. "I'll let you know if I think you're taking advantage."

She knew he would. Maybe she was afraid to put any pressure on their relationship, any more than was already there.

Shane mounted the stool, lifted the box with one hand, and with his other hand, scooped up the contents that had spilled out. Jumping off the stool, he laid the papers on the top step. One of the photographs floated to the carpet.

Hope picked it up, recognizing it immediately. It was a picture of her and Shane taken the day they'd become engaged. Had she subconsciously left this box for last? She knew what else was in it. Her gaze went to the step stool the same time as Shane's. A wedding invitation lay there. Their wedding invitation.

Venturing into frozen territory, Hope laid the photograph on top of the invitation. "The night I called off the wedding—"

"Hope, this won't do any good."

"Please let me tell you, Shane. It might help you understand."

When he remained silent, she took that as a sign he'd listen. "That night when I came in, I heard you and Mom. The doctor had just told me I was pregnant. I heard Mom ask you why you felt the way you did about children. Your response was so vehement, so absolute, that I knew if you couldn't accept children, I couldn't marry you."

"You didn't tell me you were carrying *our* child."

"But, Shane . . ."

"Like I said, Hope. This won't do any good." He glanced at the shelf in the closet. "There's nothing else up there. If you need any more help, I'll be downstairs."

She needed Shane. She needed him to open his heart to her as he'd opened it to his son.

A short while later, Hope heard the telephone ring downstairs. She had unplugged the phone in her mother's bedroom, so she was unable to answer it. From the foot of the stairs, Shane called, "Hope, it's for you."

She couldn't imagine who would be calling her, unless it was Mr. Gunthry. "I'm coming."

She hurried down the stairs. Before she lifted the receiver to her ear, Shane said, "It's a guy named Mark."

Hope smiled. Mark was a good friend and had been her next-door neighbor in Wasco. Sinking onto the floor where the phone lay, she crossed her legs under her.

Shane was almost finished removing furniture from the living room to the garage. All that remained were the end tables and coffee table. He concentrated on them now, making sure nothing was left in the small drawers. He listened, not feeling guilty in the least. The past few weeks, he'd felt as if his life had been turned upside down. The more he saw Christopher, the more time he wanted to spend with him. Each time he left his son, he didn't like the feeling.

There was only one solution to not leaving Christopher... having Christopher live with him. But he couldn't take a child from his mother. Besides, there were no grounds. From what Shane could see, Christopher came first with Hope. Always.

Of course, there was another solution. He could marry Hope. After all, she'd taken care of their son and, from what he could tell, she had done a very good job. She'd raised him alone and Shane knew that couldn't have been easy. On the other hand, she could have picked up the phone at any time. Why hadn't she?

He wondered about her decision to stay in L.A. Was she doing it for herself, for him, for Christopher? Was she staying out of guilt? Where Hope was concerned, there were too many questions and not enough answers. He didn't know if he could believe what she told him. He didn't know if he could believe her about anything important ever again.

The problem was, whenever he came within two feet of her...

"Hi, Mark. I meant to call but things have been hectic... Thanksgiving? I hope to get back sooner than that to pick up the boxes I left with Mr. Jenkins." She glanced sideways at Shane as if she wished he wasn't within hearing distance.

Tough. He was staying. Hope had driven back to Wasco, returning with a full car. The boxes were stacked in Eloise's garage. Neither Hope nor Christopher had ever mentioned anyone named Mark. Who was the guy?

"No, I know we didn't have much since the place was furnished," Hope said. "I left a few boxes I couldn't fit into the car. Mr. Jenkins was great. He prorated the month." She listened for a moment. "If you could do that, it would save me another trip up. I'll send you a money order so you can ship them. You have my aunt's address?" She smiled and listened again.

"Christopher is fine. He hasn't mentioned yet what he wants for Christmas. A fire engine? I'm sure he'd love it. I've been trying to get Mom's estate in order but now I'll concentrate on him and the holidays.... Sure you can talk to him. Hold on." She cupped her hand over the receiver. "Christopher. Mark wants to tell you something."

Shane watched his son run to the phone, eager to talk to the man on the other end of the line. While Hope looked on, Christopher chattered to Mark about his aunt, the ice-cream cone he'd had yesterday and finally said, "I have a daddy now." He held out the receiver to his mother.

Hope took the phone. "Yes, I did. I wasn't going to get into that now." She glanced up at Shane. "Yes, everything's fine. I'll write or call when we're more settled." After a few more minutes of conversation, she hung up. After Christopher ran to the kitchen to be with Eloise, Shane asked, "Who's Mark?"

Hope rose from the floor. "He was a neighbor... and friend."

"How much of a friend?"

"He's going to send the few remaining boxes so I don't have to drive back up."

"Have you known him long?"

"Ever since I moved to Wasco."

"He's not married, I take it."

"No. Divorced."

"Were you ever lovers?" Shane figured if he shocked her, she'd tell him the truth.

Hope took a deep breath, more astonished by Shane's question than anything else. As the astonishment wore off, annoyance took its place. Most of the time, Shane acted as if he didn't want anything to do with her. Now he wanted to know about her love life? His interest intrigued her and also gave her hope. Because if he cared...

"Why does it matter if I was involved with Mark?"

Gold sparks flashed in his eyes. "So you were."

"I didn't say that. I want to know why you care."

"Because what you do affects our son. I want to know if this man was in and out of your apartment as if it were his, if he stayed overnight—"

"All right," Hope broke in, deciding that answering him was the lesser of all evils. "Mark and I were never lovers. After Christopher was born, he helped me out a lot. We even dated for a while. But we both knew we were meant to be friends, nothing else."

"Only friends?"

She'd said it once, she wasn't going to say it again.

But Shane kept probing. "Does he know about us?"

All she could do was be honest with Shane and hope he would eventually believe her. "Yes. He knows Christopher is yours. I didn't see him when I went back to pack up so I didn't have a chance to tell him I'd told you about Christopher."

"Why did he call?"

Hope knew Shane was showing too much interest to merely be concerned about what had happened in Wasco. She almost smiled. Almost. "He wanted to know if Christopher would like a fire engine for Christmas."

Shane was exasperated with himself for caring who Mark was, how close he'd been to Hope and what he meant to her now. He didn't like the idea of another man buying his son gifts, of another man helping Hope after the birth of *his* son. Yet guilt stabbed him, too. As Christopher's father, *he* should be thinking about what his son wanted for Christmas. And about how to make their first Christmas together special.

He tried to put aside the topic of Hope's romantic past. "Have you bought Christopher anything yet?"

She shook her head. "No. I've got to get organized."

"Maybe you and I could go Christmas shopping some night. After the auction."

Hope gave him a radiant smile that could light up all of L.A. "I'd like that."

When she smiled like that, he remembered all the good times. He hadn't looked forward to Christmas in a very long while. A child always made Christmas special. A child and . . . a family. He wanted his son to feel the stable solidity of a family. Shane moved away from the furniture and closer to Hope. "I'd like to make Christmas special this year for Christopher."

"So would I."

The pulse at Hope's throat fluttered, and he could count each beat. The round neckline of her T-shirt just gave him a brief glimpse of the soft skin above her breasts. He remembered the softness, the suppleness, the heat when he'd aroused her.

"I'd better finish upstairs," she murmured.

On impulse, Shane laid his hand on her arm. "Come with me to the garage. See if everything is set up the way you want it."

She studied his hand on her arm, then lifted her gaze to his. "All right." As he took his hand away, she looked around the empty room. "This is so hard."

"You can cancel the auction."

"And do what? Put it all in storage? No. I can't afford it. Anyway, I have to let go. I have Mom's china and her perfume bottle collection. The rest..." Hope shrugged. "It's not going to help me remember her better."

Shane wasn't so sure of that. Hope was putting up a brave front, but getting rid of her mother's things hurt her. He wished he could make it easier somehow. He knew how loss hurt, how it lasted. He didn't want her to regret not keeping those things that were dear to her mother.

In the garage, Hope examined each piece of furniture sitting around the perimeter. "I'm giving Mom's sideboard buffet to Aunt El. She was with her when she bought it."

As Hope talked, she slowly crossed to an old-fashioned cherry vanity. The bench was covered in needlepoint. Sitting on it, she lovingly ran her fingers over the carved handles of the small vanity drawers. "I remember sitting and watching Mom while she put on her perfume and jewelry. When I played dress-up, she'd sit me on the bench and help me apply lipstick. Then she'd say, 'You can only keep it on for a little while. Remember, you're only pretending to be grown-up. You shouldn't wear lipstick until you're sixteen.'"

Shane saw the tears glisten in Hope's eyes. "Why don't you keep the vanity?"

Raising her head, Hope met his gaze in the mirror. "Where would I put it?"

"I can keep it for you. In my guest room. When you get settled somewhere, you'll have it." Though the idea of her settling somewhere other than with him was disconcerting.

It shouldn't be. She'd left him. She'd lied to him. He didn't trust her. Still, the idea of her and Christopher being someplace else, maybe moving someplace else, increased the ache in his heart.

Hope's bottom lip quivered, and he could tell she was fighting tears. Finally, she managed to say, "I would like to keep this."

He said brusquely, "Consider it done. I'll ask Jana or Adam if I can borrow their van tonight."

Rising from the bench, Hope came toward him. He wasn't sure what she was going to do until she did it. Standing on tiptoe, she kissed him gently on the cheek. It was as light as the whisper of an angel—the softness of her lips, the slight brush of her breast against his arm, the sweet smell of her—and it was over faster than he could blink. But he felt all of it in every fiber of his being.

"Thank you, Shane. Your help and understanding mean a lot to me."

The urge to draw her into his arms was so strong, he could imagine tasting her. But there was still too much between them—too many doubts, too much history.

He ignored the sting of desire and let Hope turn away. He thought again about asking her to marry him. Then he swore to himself that this time he was going to be careful. He wouldn't let her steal his heart again.

Chapter Three

Evening shadows fell across Shane as Eloise answered his knock. "Shane. Hope's not here. Was she expecting you?"

"No. I thought I'd drop by and take her and Christopher for ice cream." He also wanted to tell her that he'd set up an expense fund for Christopher. Getting to know his son had been his main preoccupation during the last few weeks. But yesterday after the auction, he'd realized the proceeds from it wouldn't last Hope very long.

"You can come in if you'd like. She had a few errands."

"Christopher went with her?"

"Those two are inseparable. I guess it's because... hmm, well ... it doesn't matter. Anyway, they shouldn't be too much longer. It's almost Christopher's bedtime."

"You don't mind if I wait? I have a few things I'd like to discuss with Hope."

"Of course I don't mind. I like the company. I'm going to miss those two when they move out. But I know Hope. As soon as she finds a job, she'll find a place of their own."

A place of their own. The two of them are inseparable.
Shane's heart ached, the same ache he'd felt since he'd seen
Hope again, since she'd told him they had a son, since he'd
become attached to his son. He hated not being able to see
Christopher anytime, day or night. He hated feeling like the
third wheel.

"I'm watching an old movie," Eloise explained. "Care to
join me? Or would you rather play gin rummy?"

Shane smiled. "Think you can beat me?"

"Any day." She motioned toward the kitchen table. "Pull
up a chair and we'll see who really knows how to play."

At first, time passed quickly as Eloise rejoiced in her luck,
calling it skill. She won the first game. And the second...because Shane was getting restless. Glancing at the
clock became more important than the cards in his hand.

Finally, after Eloise won another round, he snapped his
cards on the table. "Where did you say Hope went?"

"I think she said she might start Christmas shopping."

Was she going to do that without him? She'd said they
could shop for Christopher together. With their son along,
she couldn't be buying much.

At nine-thirty, Shane went to the front door and looked
out. Black. Everything was black. He didn't like the feeling
in his gut. Eloise came up behind him.

"Does she usually stay out this late?" he asked.

Eloise shook her head. "No. She's particular about
Christopher's bedtime."

"She seemed to get through the auction okay yesterday.
Was she more upset than she let on?"

"I don't think so. Oh, there were some tears because she
misses Jennie and yesterday was difficult, but she talked to
many of the people who bought her mother's things. She
told me afterward she felt they were the type to cherish
them."

"She wouldn't have gone back to Wasco."

"Not without telling me."

He wasn't so sure of that. With Mark there, and if she was upset, looking for comfort... "Do you have Mark what's-his-name's number?"

"I think she has her address book with her. Shane, what are you thinking?"

"I don't know what to think. I'm going to look for her."

"That would be like looking for a needle in a haystack."

"My son is out there somewhere!"

Eloise patted Shane's shoulder. "And probably perfectly safe. Do you think Hope would take any chances?"

"Eloise, I know what the streets are like. All of them. Nowhere is safe. Damn! I'm going to call Jana."

If Eloise wondered why, she didn't ask.

But Jana and Adam weren't home, either. Shane left a message, giving Eloise's number. Then he paced.

Finally, at ten-thirty, they heard a car pull into the driveway. Shane flung open the door and ran out. Hope opened her door and looked up, obviously surprised to see him.

He gulped in a deep breath. Christopher was safe; he could see him sleeping in his car seat. Hope was safe. *So don't fly off the handle.* Right. As if he hadn't been sweating buckets since nine o'clock.

"Do you need help?" he asked Hope gruffly.

"Christopher's asleep. If you could carry him to the bedroom, I'll get the packages."

Packages. She was worried about the damn packages. "Are you all right?" His gaze appraised her, noting her clothes weren't mussed or torn.

"I'm fine. We had a flat tire. I thought I could fix it myself but the lugs were too tight. By the time a patrol car stopped and called the auto club, it was nine-thirty. I didn't mean to worry anyone."

Worry. More like panic and fear. He hated the way those emotions made him feel helpless and out of control.

Shane carried Christopher to the bedroom and couldn't sit still long enough to help Hope undress their son or tuck him in. He needed air. Lots of it.

As Hope removed Christopher's shoes, Shane said, "I'll be on the front porch. Come out when you're finished."

Hope's wide blue eyes held a hundred questions, but he didn't have the answers. Standing on the porch, looking out into the blackness, knowing the terrors that lurked out there, he suddenly had one answer. The most important one.

He hadn't wanted another child. But now he was a father again. That was the reality.

So how could he best safeguard Christopher and prepare him for life?

By giving him a stable home and two parents who would put their son first. He and Hope could do that most effectively under the same roof. How stable could Christopher's life be if they were constantly trying to coordinate two households, two schedules, two sets of rules? He and Hope needed to parent together.

If they got married, Hope wouldn't have to worry about finding a job. She could stay home with Christopher and be a full-time mother. And he would have constant access to his son—not just part-time fathering.

A marriage for Christopher's sake made perfect sense. Now all he had to do was persuade Hope. But why shouldn't she agree? She wouldn't have to worry about finances or the future. Maybe this was why she'd returned—because raising a son was too difficult to handle on her own. If that was the case, she might jump at the offer of marriage.

The minutes passed like years as Shane waited. When Hope stepped onto the porch, a sweater thrown over her shoulders, his heart pounded.

"Shane, Aunt El said you were really worried. If I could have called, I would have."

"I understand." He looked up at a sky devoid of stars. "Marry me, Hope."

Hope's heart raced so fast she could hardly breathe. This proposal of Shane's, if that's what it was, was nothing like his first proposal four years ago. That one had been romantic and gentle, a question amid yellow roses and candlelight. Now he was standing in the black of night and his proposal was anything but romantic.

Yet maybe he still had feelings for her. Maybe the love hadn't died. "Why do you want to get married?" she asked softly, almost afraid to hear his reply.

He didn't hesitate, and his expression said the answer should be obvious. "To give Christopher a stable life—two parents, a home where he feels safe and secure."

"And what about us?" She held her breath.

"Us?" He looked up to the sky again, and then with a frown he faced her. "I don't know about us."

As close as they were, she could smell the familiar scent of the soap he used. Its clean, masculine aroma was as recognizable to her as the sound of his voice. Did he want to marry her only because of Christopher? Or did he still have feelings for her? Would he want her to share his bed?

"Do you intend... I mean—" She didn't know a subtle way to ask if he wanted to make love with her.

"Just because we're living together doesn't mean we have to sleep together," he said quietly.

He must be a lot stronger than she was or maybe she'd hurt him so badly when she'd called off the wedding that he no longer desired her. Yet Shane was a sensual man... with needs. "If we're married, what do you expect?"

The intensity of his stance and expression didn't change. "I expect you to make a home for us and to be faithful to our marriage, just as I will."

"But if we're not sleeping together—"

"Celibacy is nothing new to me. I haven't been a monk, but in this day and age I've been very careful. I hope you have, too."

"The right person never came along...a man I'd want to be intimate with."

Shane's stare bored into her even in the shadows. "Are you saying I'm the first and only man you've ever been with?"

"Yes."

His gaze skimmed over her from head to toe. "I wish I could believe you."

"I wouldn't lie to you, Shane."

He turned away from her, toward the house next door. "But you did. You didn't tell me the real reason for calling off the wedding, and you didn't tell me I had a son. Once trust is broken, Hope, it's real hard to fix."

She almost felt as if he couldn't stand to look at her, and that hurt. "I wish you could understand."

Facing her again, he admitted, "I can't. All I know is, nothing on this earth will keep me away from Christopher. I want legal rights to him and marrying you will give me those. As for the rest, we'll take one day at a time."

When she'd canceled their wedding, she'd hurt Shane deeply. He'd trusted her with his past and his future and he felt as if she'd betrayed that trust. She never meant to. She'd thought she loved him enough to do what was best for him. But she realized she'd been wrong not to tell him about her pregnancy, not to tell him about Christopher.

She'd always respected Shane's sense of right and wrong, the code of ethics he followed. She would trust him with her life and their son's. She remembered their Friday nights, the yellow rose that had symbolized their growing relationship, the bond that had developed from the first moment they'd talked. Shane was a strong man and sometimes too stoic and silent. But when he let his guard down, when he cared about someone, no man could be more compassionate or caring.

One evening, soon after they'd started dating, Jennie Franklin had dropped her wedding band down the drain in the kitchen. It had slipped off as she'd rinsed dishes. Shane had rolled up his sleeves and worked for two hours until he found the ring trapped in a section of pipe under the sink. He had realized what that wedding band meant to her mother.

When Hope backed out of their wedding, thinking she was giving Shane what he wanted, she'd felt as if her heart had been torn from her. Loving him still, marrying him now could make her feel whole again.

Did he still love her? Could she accept his proposal if he was only offering it because of Christopher? Yes, because she still loved him. One day at a time with Shane would be better than one day at a time without him. Eventually, he'd trust her again. She'd see to that. Eventually, he'd realize how much she loved him and then, maybe he'd feel love again, too. And together they would parent their son. If she hadn't been so young, if she hadn't been so afraid marriage to Shane and a child he hadn't wanted would kill their love, she would have married him four years ago. But the past was past. All she could do was make up for it the best she could.

"Yes, Shane. I'll marry you. On one condition."

His voice was wary. "What?"

"Any decision about Christopher's well-being we make together. No unilateral decisions—on anything." She knew how strong-minded Shane could be. She wasn't about to let him take away any of her rights as a mother.

He studied her for what seemed like hours. "All right. I agree." Extending his hand, he waited for her to take it.

As she placed her hand in his, she was aware of the largeness of his, the firmness, the strength that was so much a part of him. That strength had led him to see the straight and narrow since he was a child. Shane might not trust her, but she trusted him.

He shook her hand quickly, then let go. But for that transitory moment, she felt connected to him, and that connection gave her hope.

* * *

A week later, Eloise zipped up the back of Hope's dress and smiled at her in the dresser mirror. The dress was the palest pink satin, straight and unadorned except for a swath of tiny seed pearls across each shoulder. The sleeves were short and puffed, emphasizing the sweetheart neckline.

Holding the bouquet of white roses and baby's breath her aunt handed her, Hope looked like a bride.

The problem was, she didn't feel like a bride. "Aunt El, am I doing the right thing?"

Her aunt, dressed in mauve lace, straightened her sash. "You've loved Shane for a long time."

"But I'm afraid he doesn't love me anymore. He loves Christopher. He's patient and gentle, and it's so hard to believe he didn't want to be a father again. But at times, he tries not to even look at me. I see the pain when he looks at me, and sometimes even when he looks at Christopher. What kind of life are we going to have if he's only marrying me because of our son?"

"Child, there's still time to call this off. Is that what you want to do?"

Hope ran it all through her mind again, just as she had done so many times since she'd shaken Shane's hand, since she'd felt her love for Shane grow each time she saw him with their son, since she'd seen a doctor and asked for birth control pills. If she called off the wedding, she would lose Shane. She knew that as well as she knew her name. She just wished she had a guarantee that time *would* heal. Today, her worst fear was that Shane was marrying her only for Christopher's sake, not because he still loved her. Could that be a basis for a marriage?

Yes, it could. For this marriage. She had to believe Shane would come to love her again. Did she want to call off the ceremony? No.

Shaking her head so vigorously that her pearl earrings swung and the pearl comb in her hair slipped a bit, she said, "I don't want to call it off. I want to marry Shane."

"Then square your shoulders, hold your head high and walk over to those stairs like the lady I know you are."

Hope hugged her aunt. "I'm glad you're here. I just wish Mom could be here, too."

As Eloise leaned back, she said, "Your mother's here, Hope. Guiding you a little differently from when she was alive, but guiding you, just the same."

Hope kissed her aunt's cheek. "Thank you."

Eloise gave her a tight squeeze as they heard the music begin. Hope knew it was a tape player, but she didn't care. This was her wedding day, and she would make the most of it.

Shane stood in the living room beside Adam Hobbs, his best man. Christopher, who held a white satin pillow, rocked from one foot to the other at the foot of the stairs, waiting for his mother. Two gold bands lay on the top of the pillow. When Shane had asked Hope what kind of ring she preferred, the band was what she'd picked. She could have had anything she wanted. He'd pointed out several that were channel-set with diamonds. But she'd shaken her head and asked if he'd wear one, too. Why not? After all, they were getting married.

Beside him, Adam asked in a low voice so the minister a few feet away couldn't hear, "Are you having second thoughts?"

"No."

"You don't have to marry her to get legal rights to Christopher."

"I know. You've explained that already." Adam wasn't only Jana's husband, and a good friend. He was also a corporate attorney, who was informed about custody law be-

cause of his own situation with his two daughters from a
previous marriage.

Shane's friend kept his voice low. "I want you to make
sure you know what you're doing."

Getting married. Shane supposed to most people it meant
faith in the future. He had thought it meant that to Mary
Beth, but then she'd walked out when they should have
pulled together. Not that he blamed her. She couldn't forgive him for Davie's death, and she certainly couldn't forget it.

Shane had wanted to start fresh when he'd met Hope,
maybe so he could begin to forget, himself. Hope had given
him the chance to do that...for a few months. Then she'd
broken her promise to marry him. She'd left when, in a
sense, he'd needed her most. He wouldn't need her, or any
woman, again. He would concentrate on Christopher despite the pain, maybe because of it, and he'd take care of
Hope because she was his son's mother.

He looked over at Christopher. "I know what I'm doing," Shane responded in a decisive tone that he realized
wouldn't reassure Adam. But reassuring his best man was
low on his list of priorities.

"Shane, a child isn't enough to hold a marriage together.
You can be a good parent without marrying Hope Franklin."

Taking his gaze from his son, Shane faced Adam. "I want
to be a full-time father. I've seen what happens to kids
whose parents are split. Remember, I spend most Sundays
at the community center. I work with kids who are looking
for approval wherever they can get it, even if it means be-
longing to a gang. I want better for my son. I want better
than I had. I want to keep him safe."

"My girls are doing just fine."

Shane didn't mean to insult Adam or insinuate he was
doing something wrong. "Your situation is the exception,

and you know it. Just stand up for me, Adam. I don't need your advice."

"That's a matter of opinion," Adam muttered.

Long ago, Shane had learned he couldn't please everyone, not even the people he cared about. He could only do what he thought was right. That's the way he'd lived his life. Being a cop had reduced his vision to black and white. Shades of gray could have gotten him killed. Giving a person the benefit of the doubt, feeling pity for someone, had brought down more than one good man. Even in his capacity as a private investigator the fact had been driven home again and again—there was truth and there were lies. Husbands cheated on wives, wives cheated on husbands, con artists scammed women, white-collar thieves tried to take advantage of the system. Truth usually found the lie. But right didn't always win over wrong. He thought about Davie and felt the familiar pain.

He glanced around the room, looking for a distraction. Jana smiled at him. What Shane liked about his investigative work with Jana was the sincerity of it, the truth of it, the rightness of it. They helped people find other people. He didn't have to think about black and white.

As the music swelled, Shane turned his attention again to the stairs. Eloise came down the steps first. Christopher grinned and waved at her. His pillow tilted and Shane was glad Eloise had pinned the rings to it.

Then Hope appeared on the steps, and Shane felt as if someone had smacked him in the solar plexus with a fist. She was a vision—pink, softness, innocence. What kind of marriage could they have when he felt such mixed feelings about her?

For the past four years, he'd thought about her when his defenses were down or in the dead of night or when he came home to an empty house after a business trip. He'd thought about their months together, that one night...

Hope had been a virgin when they'd made love so he'd never had a doubt Christopher was his son. Christopher's birth date coincided with that night exactly. What Shane didn't understand was how Hope could have thrown away what they'd shared, how she could have run out on him, how she could have kept his son from him for so long.

Even though their courtship had been a whirlwind of emotions and passion, he'd thought he'd known Hope, despite their different views of the world—hers slightly naive because of her youth, his more cynical because of his age and experience. At the time, the ten-year age difference hadn't mattered. He'd fallen in love with Hope because of her fresh enthusiasm, her optimism. But now he realized he hadn't known her at all.

He was marrying a stranger.

His bride paused at the bottom step and took her son's hand. Her smile said she was not at all perturbed that Christopher hadn't stayed in his spot beside Shane. Hope's smile did as much to arouse Shane as did her curves, subtly outlined by the satin of her dress. When she faced him, her smile faded.

Shane turned toward the minister, ready to listen to the words that would change his life.

The ceremony took mere minutes. A greeting. Vows. The exchange of rings. Hope's eyes glistened, and again Shane wondered who she was and what the future would bring. He wasn't thinking beyond a life with his son, beyond the chance to nurture and safeguard this little boy, in a way he hadn't been able to nurture and protect Davie.

At the end of the ceremony, the silver-haired minister said, "You may now kiss the bride."

Shane looked down into Hope's sky blue eyes. Eloise, Adam, Christopher and Jana—who was cuddling her baby—waited expectantly. Hope's perfume wafted around him. Her soft skin beckoned him. Her dress asked for his touch. He pressed his hand against the small of her back as he bent his head. The brush of his lips on Hope's was fleeting, a heartbeat, but enough to shake the foundation of his control.

Straightening quickly, he stepped away. He would not give in to desire that could lead to heartache. He would not show Hope he was vulnerable where she was concerned. He would not give up his heart another time.

Eloise hugged Hope and kissed her as the minister shook Shane's hand. After Adam and Jana congratulated the couple, Eloise announced, "Refreshments are in the dining room. Help yourselves to punch while the bride and groom cut the cake."

Standing close by his side, Hope murmured to Shane, "If you don't want to do this, we don't have to."

The pink of her dress matched the blush on her cheeks. "Your aunt went to a lot of trouble. Let's not disappoint her." He crossed to the dining room and the cake on the table, and waited for Hope to join him.

After he passed her the knife, he covered her hand with his as they cut through the layers. When he withdrew his hand, Hope managed to shift the slice to a white paper plate. She broke off a piece and held it between her thumb and forefinger, then offered him the rest. He, too, broke off a piece, and brought it close to her mouth.

As Hope's fingers came closer to Shane's lips, he fed her. She opened her mouth, and he placed the cake inside. Her lips touched his fingers, and he felt the velvet softness of her tongue. His breath hitched, but he didn't have time to do anything but open his mouth. Somehow her finger got caught between his lips.

She pulled away, but not before he vividly remembered tasting her lips and her neck and...

Hope's world reeled. The taste of cake, icing and Shane was enough to make her dizzy. The man beside her was her husband, but he didn't seem happy about it. The past week he'd been remote, and today was no different. Shane had always been an introvert, but now he seemed even more distant—at least with her. With Adam and Jana, and even with her aunt, he didn't appear to have a problem making conversation. And certainly not with his son. But with her...

She and Shane both took a step back as if the cake and the meaning behind the tasting of it were too incendiary to accept. She saw Adam exchange a look with his wife, and she wondered what Shane had told the couple about this marriage.

Christopher sidled up beside Hope. "Cake, Mommy?"

As it had for the past four years, Hope's focus shifted to her son. She tweaked his nose, grateful for the surge of love that always filled her when she looked at him.

The reception didn't last long. Without Eloise's conversational maneuvers and Christopher's chattering, the hour or so would have been awkward. The minister left first, then Adam and Jana. Shane tugged open his tie, unbuttoned his charcoal suit coat and shrugged it off. He tossed it over a chair and rolled up his shirtsleeves. "Where are your suitcases?"

Hope touched the pearls on her shoulder. "Wait until I change and I'll help you."

His gaze slid over her. "That's not necessary." He crooked his finger at Christopher, who came running, the white jacket that matched his pants flapping as he ran. "How would you like to get out of these clothes and get comfortable before we go home?" he asked his son.

Hope crouched beside the three-year-old. "Remember I told you we're going to move in with your daddy?"

Christopher nodded then stuck one finger in his mouth and talked around it. "An' I c'n bring Teddy?"

Shane also bent down to his son's level. "You sure can. And your cars and everything else, too. My house will be your new home."

Christopher looked at Hope. "We're gonna live with Daddy and see Aunt El—but not Nana. Nana's in heaven."

After an awkward moment, Shane said, "Yes, she is." He clasped his son's shoulder. "Would you like to go pick out a swing for my backyard?"

The three-year-old took his finger from his mouth and broke into a grin. "Yeah!"

Shane smiled, adding, "And when we do get to my house, there's a surprise for you."

"What?"

With a wink, he ruffled his son's hair. "You'll just have to wait and see."

"Soon?"

"As soon as you change clothes and we pick out a swing."

Christopher grabbed Hope's hand. "C'mon, Mommy. Change."

"I have to clean up...."

Apparently, Eloise had overheard the conversation. "I'll take care of the cups and crumbs. Go on. The sooner you change, the sooner you can begin your new life."

Hope looked down at her son who couldn't wait for his surprise. If only starting a new life were that easy.

Not only did they shop for a swing set, but Shane let Christopher pick out a sliding board and jungle gym, too. While their son tried out the swing displayed in the store's parking lot, Hope nudged Shane's elbow. "Try not to go overboard." His shoulders stiffened and his jaw set. She realized she should have been more tactful. "I just mean—"

"Hope, I will buy my son anything I damn well please."

Patiently, she returned, "A swing set and jungle gym won't make your house into a home."

"A swing set, jungle gym and anything else Christopher might enjoy will help him feel comfortable. Just because you might not have been able to give him everything you wanted to, doesn't mean I can't."

"Shane, we have an agreement."

"Yes, we do. I did not make a unilateral decision. You're here with me."

"But you're not listening."

"I heard you. You want me to *not* buy Christopher a jungle gym because it will make you feel better in some way. Tell me why he shouldn't have it."

"I don't want you to spoil him. I don't want you to think buying him presents will make you a father!" As soon as she said it, she regretted it.

Shane's voice was cold as he answered her. "I expect I can read some books on the subject since my practical experience is lacking. We both know why it's lacking, so maybe you should take that into consideration when I want to buy my son something."

There was nothing Hope could say to that, nothing to defend her position. She couldn't prevent Shane from wanting to make up for the years he'd missed. Shane didn't wait for a response from her, but strode toward Christopher, then waited for him to jump off the swing and climb onto the glider attached to the crossbar.

Hope watched them together—father and son—and wished she had never run away, wished she had faced Shane with the truth before Christopher was born. Shane's resentment then couldn't have been any worse than his anger now.

A short time later, whether Shane wanted her help or not, Hope carried the last of her belongings into his house. She had brought her car over yesterday, and Shane had driven her and Christopher to Eloise's last evening.

Shane took her suitcase and garment bag to the second-floor guest room at the end of the hall. Christopher followed on his daddy's heels, lugging a small carryall that contained his miniature cars.

After Hope set her cosmetics case on the dresser, she hung her wedding dress in the closet.

Shane beckoned to Christopher. "C'mon, sport. I'll show you your surprise."

Christopher ran down the hall after Shane. Hope heard, "Look, Mommy. Come look!"

As curious as her son, she quickly followed him and stood in the doorway of the second guest bedroom, surveying the interior which had changed drastically since she'd seen it last. "When did you do this?"

"The furniture came this morning."

A youth bed with a bookcase headboard stood against one wall. A table with four chairs, Christopher's size, was placed beside a chalkboard and toy box in the shape of a football. A toy bulldozer and steamroller decorated the shelves where a variety of books also waited.

Christopher opened the toy box. "Wow! Cars and..." He lifted out a purple dinosaur. "Barney!"

Shane's lean face showed obvious joy over Christopher's pleasure. His gaze connected with Hope's. She walked over to the bed. "Think you'll like sleeping here?"

"You'll be over there?" He pointed to the room where Shane had deposited the suitcases.

"Yes, I will. And your daddy will be right across the hall. I brought your night-light, too. We'll plug it in before you go to bed."

Christopher sat on the bed and bounced a few times, obviously happy with his room.

Hope smiled and Shane smiled back. The simple exchange made her feel better about the wedding that didn't seem like a wedding, about the separate bedrooms, about their past.

Shane asked Hope, "Where would you like to go for supper?"

"That's up to you," she deferred, still feeling her way, not knowing what Shane had in mind.

"There's a nice restaurant a few miles from here. Quiet, stained-glass windows. The service is good. I don't think it would be too long for Christopher to sit. Or if you'd like, we can order and I'll go get it."

"I'd like to go out. Especially since it's our wedding day," she said quietly.

Shane's brown eyes darkened.

"Do I need to change?"

His jaw tensed as he surveyed her royal blue blouse and slacks. "You're fine the way you are. I'll change and we can go."

Hope had always felt as if Shane could see right through her. Since she knew he knew what was underneath the clothes, she couldn't prevent the heat flushing her cheeks.

Shane didn't comment but went into his bedroom, a room she'd shared with him one night long ago.

Christopher's day had been a long, exciting one. His eyelids started to droop by dessert, and he fell asleep in the car on the way home. Shane carried Christopher up to his new room and Hope undressed the little boy while Shane found a pair of pajamas in the suitcase.

"Sleepy, Mommy," Christopher grumbled.

"I know, honey. Let's go to the bathroom and then you can crawl right into bed."

Shane helped Hope put Christopher into his pajamas. He held a sleeve as Hope guided the little boy's hand through. While she buttoned up the shirt, he plugged the night-light into the receptacle by the window.

Hope found Christopher's teddy bear at the foot of the bed and tucked the toy in beside the little boy. Then she leaned close and kissed his cheek. "Good night, little one. Happy dreams."

Hope saw Shane look down at his son and brush Christopher's fine brown hair across the child's forehead before following her into the hall and down the stairs. She wasn't sure what to do next. Conversation seemed preferable to the awkward silence. There was something she knew she had to say. "Thank you for Christopher's room."

His eyebrows arched as if her thank-you surprised him. "You're welcome. You really think he likes it?"

"I know he does. Especially the toy box. It was thoughtful of you."

"Not excessive?"

She shook her head. "No. Shane, I'm sorry about what I said...."

Bracing his hand on the wall above her head, he admitted, "I thought about what you said, and you're right. Buying Christopher presents won't make me a father. I have a feeling getting there is going to be a matter of trial and error."

She smiled and her heart raced at Shane's closeness. She could still smell the scent of his soap mixed with his own male scent that made her stomach quiver. "Aren't most things?"

"I suppose." He straightened and towered over her. "I have some work to do that I put aside this week. I'll be in my office if you need anything."

"Oh." She couldn't hide her disappointment.

He heard it. "What?"

She shrugged. "I thought maybe we could talk for a while."

His eyebrows arched. "About?"

"Anything. Shane, this is our wedding day."

"And I'm doing the best I can with it. What do you want? Champagne and toasting each other by candlelight?"

"A toast to our future would be nice."

He ran his hand quickly over his face. "Hope, I'm still so angry about what you did—"

Before she thought better of it, she clasped his arm. "You didn't want children. Can't you understand I thought I was making the best decision for both of us?" He glanced down at her hand and she took it away, but not before she felt the muscle, the springy hair, the pure maleness of him.

"Why now, Hope? Why, after all this time, did you decide to tell me? Because you can't make it on your own?"

"No! I'm sure I can find another job, especially here. And Christopher and I have always had what we needed. I came back for lots of reasons. Over the years I've missed Dad terribly. He died at such an important time in my life—right before I started high school, when I was beginning to look at boys differently, when I had so many doubts about myself and what I wanted to do with my life. The last three years, parenting Christopher alone, I realized how difficult those years must have been for Mom. When I lost her so suddenly, I realized Christopher needed more than me, more than visiting Aunt El now and then. He needed a connection with his father if that was possible."

"You really thought I might not want that connection?"

"I honestly didn't know."

Shane looked down at her, searching her face, his gaze lingering on her lips. "You didn't know me."

"Maybe not," she whispered.

"And I never knew you. I never suspected you could hide something so important."

His brown eyes held disappointment and sadness, too much for him to disguise. When she'd walked out on him, had she killed his love for her? She bit her lip. "I'm sorry."

He shook his head. "Sorry isn't good enough. It won't make up for the years I've lost."

"What can I do?"

"That's just it, Hope. There's nothing you can do. Maybe time will help. I don't know."

She struggled to hide the emotions coursing through her, especially the way she still felt about Shane. He obviously had lost all feeling for her, except his anger and resentment. "And you think we can still have a marriage?"

He jammed his hands into the pockets of his black trousers. "We can be parents to Christopher."

"Don't *we* matter?"

"Not right now."

Fighting back tears, she made one last attempt. "At least let me be your friend."

"I trust my friends, Hope."

What he didn't say was clear. He didn't trust her. She swallowed hard, trying to ignore how much his words hurt, trying to look at their life together realistically. "I usually make breakfast around eight. Is that all right?"

He studied her for a moment. "Eight is fine. I usually just grab a cup of coffee but that might change with Christopher around. I went to the store yesterday and stocked up on everything I could think of. If you can't find something, just ask."

Her gaze met his. "I will."

Familiar gold sparks flashed in his eyes. Almost reluctantly, he reached out and brushed a stray lock of hair away from her cheek. "You looked beautiful today, Hope."

She had no answer, no murmured thank-you, because all her emotions jammed as the heat of his fingers scorched her cheek. Remembered tenderness was evident in his touch.

Dropping his hand, he said, "I'll see you in the morning."

All she could do was nod, watch him walk away and wonder if marrying him now had been an even bigger mistake than running away from him when she was twenty.

Chapter Four

"**M**ommy! Mommee—"

Hope came awake and was on her feet instantly. Without bothering to grab her robe, she dashed toward her son's cry, sliding onto his bed and holding him in her arms. "What's wrong, honey?"

The hall light went on and Shane's shadow fell across the bed. He waited there, watching Hope, watching his son.

Christopher tightened his arms around Hope's neck. "I wanna sleep wif you."

Hope hugged him then leaned away. "All right. But can you tell me why?"

"'Cause...I don' know. I just wanna sleep wif you."

"Did you have a bad dream?"

He shrugged.

"Are you afraid to sleep in here by yourself?"

He nodded.

"You have Teddy with you," she soothed.

"I wanna go wif you."

Hope combed his hair back from his forehead. "You can sleep with me if you're sure that's what you want to do. But how about if I stay here with you until you fall asleep again?"

Christopher poked his finger in his mouth and thought about it. "Okay. Can I sleep wif Barney, too?"

Shane strode across the room, plucked the purple dinosaur from the shelf and set it in Christopher's lap. His hand brushed Hope's midriff. Suddenly she was aware of the intimacy of the situation. At first, her only concern had been Christopher. Now, sitting before Shane, his bare chest sprinkled with a matt of light brown curling hair, his black silk shorts riding low on his hips, she was more aware than ever that this was their wedding night, and they were spending it in separate rooms.

She tried to speak but had to clear her throat and try again. "We'll be all right if you want to go back to bed."

His gaze flicked over her quickly, then he slowly crossed to the doorway. "Christopher, would you like me to leave the hall light on?"

The three-year-old nodded.

Shane gave his son a smile. "I'll see you in the morning."

Hope waited until Shane was back in his room before she slid down into Christopher's bed and he squiggled and snuggled with Barney and Teddy, finally settling against her. "'Night, Mommy," he murmured.

She kissed his cheek.

Hope had not intended to fall asleep. She'd planned to wait until Christopher slept before slipping back to her room. But when she opened her eyes and saw the clock on her son's shelf read 4:00 a.m., she realized she'd dozed off.

Christopher lay on his side, his dinosaur under his arm, his bear by his side. Hope sat up and swung her legs soundlessly over the side. Stopping in the doorway, she made sure her son was still sleeping.

She'd turned toward her room when Shane appeared in the hall. Startled, she jumped.

"I didn't mean to scare you," he said.

"You didn't. I just didn't expect you to still be awake."

"I heard you get out of Christopher's bed."

"I didn't make any noise."

"Squeaky floorboard," Shane explained. "In the dead of night, my instincts take over and I can't forget I was a cop once."

His brown eyes held her where she stood, though she knew she should get back to her room. His face was too close to hers, his voice too night-husky. He was danger and safety and too much man for her peace of mind as he stood within reach. Her pulse fluttered at her throat, and her nipples hardened.

Shane's gaze brushed across her lips and lingered on the neckline of her peach cotton gown. Her common sense told her to run. Her heart told her to stay. If she could make him want her again...

"Do you always give him a choice?"

"What?" Her voice came out as a whisper.

"Christopher. I thought for sure he'd want to sleep in your room, but you gave him the choice."

"He's getting more independent. If *he* makes the decision, he's usually satisfied with it. Fewer tantrums and problems in the long run."

Shane's eyebrows arched. "I can't imagine him having tantrums."

She couldn't help smiling. "You might be in for a surprise. He can be quite stubborn when he wants his own way."

"I guess I've been a playmate more than a parent. I'll try to be more aware of that. I remember Davie at that age—" He stopped abruptly. "I've watched how you talk with Christopher, how you handle him. You're a good mother, Hope."

"My mom taught me everything I know. She was the best role model I could have ever had."

"You miss her."

Hope could feel quick hot tears that she willed away. "I miss her a lot."

The nerve in Shane's jaw worked as, again, he ran his eyes over her from head to toe. When his gaze reached her bare feet, he said, "You'd better get back to bed."

She nodded but couldn't seem to move away.

He did. At his bedroom door, he paused. "Should I leave the hall light on?"

"Yes, in case he wakes up again."

Shane looked toward Christopher's bedroom. "I'll see you in the morning." With that, Shane turned, went into his room and shut the door.

Shane heard Hope walk back to her room. He sank onto his king-size bed and ran both hands through his hair. Her footsteps were so light, like an angel barely touching the earth. In that simple gown... He held out his hand. It was trembling, and he felt like a fool. Seeing her sleep-mussed hair, her pink cheeks, their son in her arms... Damn!

Dropping his hand to his knee, he remembered the way her breasts had responded to his nearness. Hope Franklin Walker was not an angel. This time he wouldn't let her get close enough to see his heart, his soul, or his desire.

He'd always been good at keeping people at bay; he'd had years of practice. First with his father. Bud Walker had been a mean drunk. Shane had learned early to stay away and show no emotion.

And with his mother... She'd become a broken woman by the time his father left. The doctors said she'd died of an overdose of sleeping pills. Shane knew better. She'd died of a shattered heart.

No, he wouldn't let Hope get close enough to do any damage. All he had to do was keep up his guard. He'd care

for and protect his son and treat Hope like a roommate.
How hard could that be?

Hope started breakfast the next morning, agonizing over
her conversation with Shane the night before, and their en-
counters in Christopher's room and the hall. Their wedding night.

She cracked an egg into a bowl. She felt Shane before she
saw him. Shivers skipped up her back and when she looked
over her shoulder, she saw the guarded look on his face. He
wore cutoff denims and a black T-shirt with the letters advertising Sea World almost washed off. He looked as tired
as she felt.

As he came to the counter where she was standing, her
heart beat faster. She said the only thing that came to mind.
"Good morning."

He lifted a mug from the wooden tree. "'Morning."

"Christopher was still sleeping when I came down," she
told him.

"When I looked in on him, he looked so peaceful. Made
me wonder what I'd have to do to sleep that soundly."

Hope didn't know whether to pursue that line of thought.
Deciding against it, she stuck to the mundane. "I'm making scrambled eggs for Christopher and me. How would you
like yours?"

"Scrambled is fine." Shane poured coffee into his mug,
his elbow brushing hers. His eyes collided with hers.

Her body pulsed with the desire to have him hold her in
his arms. Ducking her head, she cracked another egg into
the bowl. "Do you have outside appointments today?"

"Why?"

She sighed, hoping every conversation they had wouldn't
be such a struggle. "I have to go to Mom's and make one
last check. It shouldn't take long. I can take Christopher
along or I can leave him here with you."

Shane stared into his coffee, then raised his head. "Would you like me to go along?"

"You'd do that?"

Shane took a cautious sip of the hot coffee. "We're married, Hope. If you want me there, I'll go with you."

"I'd like that. Is after lunch all right?"

"That's fine." Taking his mug with him, Shane headed for his office. "Let me know when breakfast is ready."

As Shane left the kitchen, Hope wondered if he had the rules for their marriage written down somewhere. He seemed to know them. She didn't.

The next day, Hope put Christopher down for his nap feeling as if she needed one, too. Maybe the emotional upheaval from the past month had caught up with her—her mother's death, telling Shane about Christopher, the move to L.A., getting married. Yesterday, Shane had stood by her side as she walked through an empty house. She'd longed to turn to him again for comfort, but she couldn't. He was there physically, but emotionally he was hundreds of miles away. She didn't know how to reach him.

In the living room now, she heard voices coming from Shane's office—Jana must have arrived while she was upstairs. Eager to get to know Shane's partner better, Hope headed toward the sun-filled room.

As she stood in the doorway, she could see Shane standing at Jana's desk, leaning over her. His head was very near his partner's. He murmured something, and Jana laughed. His smile said he shared her humor. They seemed so easy together, so... friendly. Jealousy stabbed Hope and she knew there was no reason for it. Jana and Adam were happily married. Weren't they?

Shane laid his hand on Jana's shoulder.

Hope didn't think she'd moved or made a sound, but Jana turned toward her. "Hi there. I just stopped in to pick up some paperwork I can enter in the computer at home."

Jana's smile was pleasant, her tone friendly without a shred of guilt. Hope's gaze went to Shane's hand on his partner's shoulder. He saw the look, waited a moment, then removed it.

Jana stepped right into the awkwardness. "Hope, how would you like to go shopping with me sometime or maybe have dinner?"

The invitation was a surprise. There was a warmth that emanated from Jana, a caring that was hard to resist. "I'd like that."

"I'll check Adam's schedule and see when he can watch Matthew." She smiled. "He doesn't like to use a baby-sitter unless it's necessary."

"Where's Matthew now?" Hope asked.

"With Adam. He took the afternoon off to spend with his girls and son." Jana shuffled the papers in front of her into a pile and stood. "I'd better get going. We're having a barbecue this evening and I told Adam I'd stop at the bakery and pick something up for dessert." She pushed her chair back and took her purse from the desk top. On her way out, she said, "Hope, I'll be in touch with you about getting together."

Jana had closed the front door when Hope commented, "She seems nice."

"She's more than nice."

Hope couldn't tell if there was simply respect in Shane's voice or more. "How long have she and Adam been married?"

"It was three years in August."

"Did you know Jana before she married Adam?"

"Why all the questions, Hope?"

"I just wondered."

His eyes narrowed. "I knew Adam first."

"Oh."

"What's on your mind?"

"Nothing really. You and Jana seem . . . close."

"We're partners and we're friends."

"I see."

"But I don't. I don't think you're saying what's on your mind."

Before Hope married Shane, she'd decided she would never keep anything from him again. But telling him what she'd felt when she came in and saw him and Jana together... "I wondered what your feelings are for Jana. You seem so comfortable with her, so affectionate."

"From the moment I met Jana, I realized she brought out the best in the people she's around."

He wasn't telling her anything. She was trying to be honest and open with him, but he was more closed than ever. "Did you mind when she married Adam?"

"Adam's a good friend."

"But did you mind?" She could be just as stubborn as he was.

His eyes became piercing brown as he stood perfectly still. "No, I didn't mind. Adam and Jana are made for each other. No one could interfere in their relationship even if they tried."

He still wasn't telling her *his* feelings. "Are you attracted to Jana?"

His voice became as sharp as his eyes. "Dammit, Hope. Why the inquisition? I'm married to you."

"I'm not sure how much that means." Her words shot out unexpectedly, surprising her and Shane.

With restrained patience, he explained, "As I told you a moment ago, Jana is a partner and a friend. I like her because she's easy to be around, she's sincere and honest and can read people better than anyone I know. But that's it. I don't want her in my bed. I don't wish she and Adam weren't married. Does that satisfy your curiosity?"

The month had been too long, too fraught with emotion for her to spar with Shane now. "I wasn't curious. I was jealous." On that admission, she left Shane's office and went to the kitchen to start supper.

That night, Shane listened as Hope read Christopher a story. When she imitated the voices of Papa Bear, Mama Bear and Baby Bear, Christopher giggled and said, "Do it again, Mommy." Hope smiled and repeated that part of the story.

Her smile. Shane wanted to kiss it more than he wanted to find his newest client's lost high school sweetheart. Why did Hope have the power to get to him? It was purely physical—her smell, her taste, the sight of her. She was just a woman, a woman who'd lied to him...and left him.

When Hope finished the story, she kissed Christopher good-night. Shane gave his son a hug, then followed her down the stairs. The past two nights he'd gone to his office after they'd put Christopher to bed. It was safer that way. But tonight he had to get something straight between them.

Hope sat on the sofa in the living room and picked up a book she'd been reading the evening before. Looking up at him with surprise on her face, she asked, "You're not working tonight?"

He sat on the arm of the sofa. "In a minute. I have something to tell you first."

She frowned. "Good or bad?"

"I have to go out of town."

"A case?"

"Yes. I'm leaving Sunday evening."

"Do you go out of town often?"

"It depends on our clients. Sometimes I have to follow a lead in person."

"Jana doesn't?"

"She does when she has to. I...uh...should explain something about Jana. She's got this gift for finding people. She's psychic."

Hope was silent for a good minute. "So you use your experience and connections as a cop and she does the rest."

"Sort of. You know, if I told most people what I just told you, they would be skeptical."

Hope shrugged. "If *you* believe in Jana, why should I doubt her? You don't believe without proof."

Hope was right about that. For him, seeing was believing. "I had firsthand proof. Adam's daughters were missing, and Jana helped find them. Her gift is amazing." Hope's blue eyes clouded, and he remembered what she'd said earlier. "If it's true you're jealous, you have no reason to be . . . of Jana or anyone else. I told you I'd be faithful to our marriage, and I will be."

The clouds didn't leave her eyes. "Are you sorry you married me?"

"We haven't been married long enough to have regrets," he replied cautiously.

"Our lives are so separate, except for Christopher."

"It's got to be that way, Hope. Until we can find some common ground." Until he could begin to trust her again.

Her eyes were so blue, her expression so vulnerable. He was drawn toward common ground and Hope's softness.

She tilted her head up as he lowered his. She was everything womanly. His body responded to hers as if they'd never been apart. Her lips weren't enough. He wanted to taste her secrets, find out if she was playing some game with him, remember the ecstasy they'd once shared.

When his tongue breached her lips, she opened them freely, welcoming his desire. He didn't take time to tease, but stroked against her again and again, raising the stakes, seeing how far she'd go. It wasn't that he wanted her to stop him. Lord knew he could use the physical release. But knowing he didn't trust her, would she use sex to try to break through his defenses? Or worse yet, would she feel she owed him something because he'd married her?

Hope tried to think. The kiss had been sudden, unexpected. At the first touch of Shane's lips, her doubts faded, her dreams reawakened. Maybe he could forgive her. Maybe he finally understood why she'd left, why she'd been afraid to stay. She slipped into the world they'd shared once, where kisses and touching could make them one. Shane's lips weren't enough, neither was the sweep of his tongue. She wanted to show him they could recapture the past and forge a future.

She reached for him, her hand finding the taut planes of his back, the richness of the muscles underneath. Running her fingers up and down, she remembered and wanted more.

Abruptly, Shane broke away and growled, "That's enough, Hope."

She didn't understand his anger any more than she understood why he'd broken away. Trying to rein in her emotions, trying to make sense of the kiss and Shane's reaction, she asked, "What's wrong? We're married, Shane. I'd understand if you want—"

"What I *want* has nothing to do with this. I can't help wondering if you're willing to use sex to get closer to me, to get what *you* want."

"And what do I want, Shane?"

"That's what I'm trying to figure out. By marrying me, you got a father for Christopher and security. Do you figure giving me your body will repay the debt?"

All the breath left Hope's lungs and the room swam. This was more than a lack of trust. Shane's resentment and anger were greater than she ever imagined. "Nothing I tell you will change the way you feel. So you're going to have to figure it out on your own. But remember, I wasn't the one who started all this. Maybe you'd better decide if that kiss was a test or a disguise for something else."

She pushed up from the cushion, the emotional strength she'd developed since she'd broken up with Shane taking her up the stairs without a backward glance. She realized now they could never recapture the past. They'd have to start from scratch. The problem was—she wasn't sure at all how to start.

Hearing the key in the lock Wednesday evening, Hope pushed her knitting into the tapestry bag. It had been six days since she'd realized she and Shane had to start from square one. When Shane had gone out of town on business, she'd begun knitting him a sweater for Christmas. It was her way of believing in the future, believing that by the New Year she and Shane would have a future. But she'd also made some decisions. The first was that if desire flared between them again, Shane would have to make the first move. She had too much self-respect to let something like that happen again.

The second decision was to take a job if it was offered.

Shane came into the living room and plunked his traveling bag by the sofa.

"Did you have a good trip?"

"I'll find out tomorrow after I make some calls." He glanced toward the stairs. "Everything all right here?"

"Just fine. I put Christopher to bed about an hour ago."

His gaze slowly passed from her hair, pinned with a barrette on one side, over her lavender jumpsuit, to the length of her legs. "I'll have to make some time to spend with him tomorrow. I missed him."

So much for easing into the conversation of her getting a job. "I have an appointment tomorrow afternoon, and I've asked Aunt El to look after him. Would you like to keep him yourself?"

"Where are you going?"

"I received a call from a day-care center where I had an interview. They want me to come in again."

"I see."

Hope wasn't sure Shane really understood. She'd decided she couldn't center her life around him; she needed to have her own goals. "I might be late. The supervisor said after we talk, she'd like me to stay and see how the facility is run."

Shane shrugged. "Tell Eloise I'll keep Christopher. I'll just make something on the grill for supper."

"You're sure? If you're trying to get something else done, he can be a handful..."

"I'm capable of taking care of my son and making supper. You do it all the time."

Yes, she did. But she'd had three years of practice. She wasn't about to say that and take the lid off Pandora's box. "Would you like something before you turn in? I made a casserole for supper that I can heat up."

Shane's gaze passed over her legs once more and came to rest on her lips. "No. Food doesn't hold any appeal right now." The huskiness in his voice told her that he was thinking about the kisses they'd shared, the desire that hummed between them.

But she wouldn't sacrifice her dignity again. She would not be the one to give in to desire. Not after what Shane had said.

"Has Christopher had any more bad dreams?" he asked.

"No. But I've been leaving on the hall light." She made herself break eye contact and stand. "I'm glad you're back, Shane. Christopher and I both missed you."

He cocked his head and studied her carefully as if looking for the truth. She didn't want her every word to be suspect; she didn't want to have to watch what she said. So instead of standing there and letting him search, she said, "Good night," and headed for the stairs.

Thursday afternoon, Shane used the pruning shears on the bushes while he watched Christopher play on the swing. As he clipped the crepe myrtle, he thought about his last trip. Usually, he didn't mind traveling. But the entire time he'd been away, he'd thought about . . . Christopher—what he was doing, how he was doing it, whether he slept through the night.

"Daddy, look!" The command came from a few feet away.

Shane looked up and felt his heart stop. His son was standing, actually standing, at the top of the sliding board. Shane dropped the shears and his legs ate up the distance in seconds. Holding Christopher at the waist, he told him, "You don't stand at the top. You could fall. Sit and slide down."

Christopher's brown eyes showed surprise, then defiance. "Don't wanna sit."

"Sit down, Christopher."

"No."

The screen on the porch slammed and Hope came down the steps into the yard. She wore a cornflower blue suit, the same color as her eyes. Her white high heels were simple but showed the curves of her legs to perfection. As she came toward him, Shane took a deep breath.

Seeing his mother, Christopher sat at the top of the slide looking as angelic as any three-year-old could. Suddenly Shane realized Christopher was testing him, seeing how far he could go. Like any child, he was trying to push the boundaries as far as he could.

Hope patted her son's knee. "I have to leave or I'll be late."

"Go ahead," Shane urged, arching an eyebrow at his son. "We're fine."

Doubt flickered in Hope's eyes, but Shane had to give her credit, she didn't voice what she was thinking. She was really trying to let him develop his own relationship with his son. That couldn't be easy for her after having had him all to herself for three years.

She gave Christopher a last loving smile and a wave, then walked along the path leading to the front of the house. As the sun shone on her head, red highlights sparkled in her hair. With each step, her hips swayed and Shane felt a tightness he recognized all too well. He'd hoped his trip had given him some perspective, but his body didn't know one perspective from the other. He was attracted to Hope and he would have to live with it.

Christopher slid down the sliding board, landing unsteadily on his feet. Running around to the ladder, he climbed to the top again, and promptly stood as if daring Shane to scold him.

So much for perspective.

Four hours later, Shane glanced at his watch then back at the mess in the kitchen. Groceries lay scattered across the counter. Christopher sat on the floor in the midst of strips of unrolled paper towels, plastic containers filled with water from the bathroom sink and a variety of pots and pans. His son wore one of the lids on his head.

Hope made taking care of their son and the house look easy. It wasn't... unless she knew some secret she hadn't shared. Of course, Shane hadn't let her share much, preferring to learn about his son himself. He'd learned a bookful this afternoon. She was right about Christopher wanting his own way. If Christopher didn't have Shane's full attention, he did everything he could to get it.

The afternoon had been a battle of wills. Shane hadn't been around a lot when Davie was this age. He'd been too busy trying to make detective, trying to make the world a safer place. This afternoon, he'd realized how little he knew about disciplining a child. Davie had been an easy baby, a joyful toddler, an eager first-grader. Mary Beth had handled the discipline, and when Shane was around, Davie usually cuddled in his dad's lap for a story or simply played within reach.

Christopher was more active, wanting to do or go. He was curious in a way Davie had never been. And when that curiosity was curbed...

Shane recognized his own stubborn streak in his son, but wasn't sure how to deal with it. So he'd done the best he could by warning, cajoling, reasoning. Only, Christopher had ignored most of it, doing what he damn well pleased. Finally, Shane had let him, not knowing what else to do, especially after their nightmare trip to the grocery store.

Shane heard the front door open. He ran his hand through his hair and mentally groaned. Wouldn't Hope get a kick out of this!

He waited for her hoot of laughter or her gasp of surprise. But when she finally appeared in the doorway, she was silent. Christopher ran over to her and hugged her around the knees. His shorts were wet, his hands were sticky and there was a smudge of chocolate on his forehead from the candy bar he'd picked up at the store and insisted on eating right there.

She crouched to his level, unmindful of his sticky fingers. "Did you have a good afternoon?"

Christopher glanced guiltily at Shane but then bobbed his head.

Hope raised her chin and met Shane's gaze. "Did *you* have a good afternoon?"

"I don't think 'good' quite characterizes it." A small smile played on her mouth, and she bit her lower lip. Shane suspected she was suppressing a grin.

"I'm trying to get supper started," he said gruffly. He didn't like to be laughed at, but he deserved it after this fiasco.

"I'll take Christopher upstairs and help him get cleaned up, then I'll help you with supper."

It seemed like no time at all until Hope and Christopher returned to the kitchen. But instead of adding to the chaos, Christopher helped Hope pick up the pots, pans and paper towels. Shane had managed to wipe up most of the water. When Christopher settled on the living room floor to build with a set of blocks, Shane asked Hope, "How do you do it?"

Turning from the lettuce she was tearing apart for the salad, she asked, "Do what?"

"Watch him and get anything done!"

She didn't laugh as he suspected she might. "It took practice."

He hung a wet towel on the handle of the stove. "I could practice from now until doomsday—"

"Shane, he was testing his boundaries."

"I figured that out. I just didn't know what to do about it." Admitting that was tough for Shane. He was used to knowing what to do, rarely confused about what direction to take.

Hope sliced a carrot into the salad. "I use time-outs with Christopher."

Shane stood beside her, watching her slender fingers. "And they are...?"

"When he does something he's not supposed to do or doesn't listen, he has to sit in a specified chair for three, five, or seven minutes. I set a timer. I should have told you about it, but I thought you'd want to find your own way of dealing with him."

"In other words, you didn't think I'd listen to you."

Hope diplomatically kept silent and sliced a cucumber.

Shane mowed his hand through his hair. "I found out today how different kids are. Because I was a father once, I thought I could do it the same way. But each child is as individual as his name."

"Christopher reminds you of Davie." She said it softly, not pressing too hard.

He leaned against the counter. "Yes. But today I really saw them as two different boys. They might look alike, but Christopher is Christopher."

The only sound in the kitchen was Hope slicing the cucumber.

He realized all the things she could say, how she could resent him for not seeing Christopher as unique all along. But she kept silent. Shane remarked, "He can be a little tornado. I guess you know what works with him."

"Not all the time," she said in a tone that let him know she understood the afternoon he'd experienced.

She was letting him keep his pride, telling him subtly that she didn't have all the answers, either. But where their son was concerned, she knew a hell of a lot more than he did. "Time-outs, huh?"

She put down the knife. "Time-outs and lots of hugs. You're good with Christopher, Shane."

"Yeah, I guess I'm not too bad. The house was still standing when you got home."

She laughed at his wry humor, and he had to smile back. He also felt compelled to move closer, to breathe in the enticing scent of lingering perfume, to watch her breasts rise and fall with each breath.

Hope saw the frustration leave Shane's face, saw the golden desire flash in his eyes before he moved closer. Her hand, resting on the counter, began to tremble. She and Shane had managed to have a normal conversation. They'd worked together cleaning up and starting supper, as if they shared a common bond, as if they were working side by side like a husband and wife. And he'd realized Christopher was unique in his own right. Maybe now the pain from Davie's death would diminish and he could find joy in *this* son.

She wanted Shane to kiss her. She wanted it so much she was shaking. But what would Shane's reaction be afterward? The same as the other night?

As his head bent to hers, she knew she couldn't let him kiss her until she determined his motive. Before his lips could touch hers, she whispered, "Is this another test?"

He raised his head and frowned, his voice husky. "I guess I deserved that." Moving away as if her interruption had brought him to his senses, he said, "I'll put the hamburgers on the grill."

Hope wished she hadn't said anything, had let the kiss happen. But she couldn't take that chance, not if she wanted Shane to respect her. She had to start with that.

A few hours later, they put Christopher to bed. While Shane read their son a story, she went out on the back porch to enjoy the quiet, to let a bit of peace surround her soul. When she heard Shane's footsteps in the kitchen, she didn't expect him to come out and join her. But tonight, instead of heading to his office, he came out onto the porch.

Leaning against the wrought-iron railing, he crossed one foot over the other. He looked relaxed, but Hope knew better. Shane never did anything without a reason.

"How did the interview go today?"

The late-day warmth still lingered in the air although the temperature had dropped. With Shane standing on the porch with her, the warmth took precedence. "It went very well. I can have the job if I want it when the program director goes on maternity leave in a few months."

"I'd prefer if you don't take the job."

She sighed. "You want me to stay here with Christopher."

"Yes. Is there anything wrong with that?"

"No. But I'd feel better if I'm contributing to our income."

"You don't need to work, Hope. I can support us. It's more important that you raise our son." After a tense silence, he added, "Or do you want a job for other reasons?"

"Like...?"

"Maybe you need to stash away some money in case you want to bail out."

All she could do was reassure him, if he wanted reassurance. These days, she didn't know what he wanted. "I have no intention of bailing out. But maybe you'd like to think I will. Are you hoping I don't stay? Then your responsibility for us would be over. You could say you tried but it just didn't work."

He uncrossed his feet and straightened against the balustrade. "Don't be ridiculous. Now that I know I have a son, my responsibility toward him will never end."

"Yes, you've made that clear. My responsibility for him will never end, either."

"Your responsibilities are different. He needs you with him. And now you can be. You don't have to work."

If she relied on Shane to support them, he would suspect her motives. But if she took the job, he might resent her even more. "I have to think about it, Shane. I'll let you know what I decide."

"No unilateral decision about Christopher. Wasn't that the deal?"

"And as you told me when you bought the jungle gym, I've listened to you, and now I have to make up my own mind."

Shane pushed away from the railing and was close enough that she could see the tiny scar on his left cheekbone. Instead of angry, his voice was amazingly gentle. "When you make up your mind, try to think about what Christopher needs, not about what's going on between you and me."

She wasn't sure what was going on between her and Shane. But it would be easy to put Christopher first; she'd done that since the day she'd found out she was pregnant.

Chapter Five

On Saturday afternoon, Shane's headband caught the sweat as he dribbled the basketball around Adam, aimed and shot. The ball danced around the rim, teetered and fell over the side. Shane swore, grabbed for the ball to rebound, but Adam was quicker.

He dribbled the ball in front of his opponent. "Playing hard today, aren't you?" Adam asked.

Shane swayed back and forth, ready to guard, ready to jump. "I'm playing like I always play—to win."

Adam went for the basket, but Shane blocked him, almost knocking them both over as he grabbed for the ball. Adam stooped with his hands on his thighs and took a deep breath. "Let's say you win and give it a rest."

Shane shook his head. "Uh-uh. I need the workout. Getting too old for this?" he needled.

Adam suddenly stole the ball from his friend and casually dribbled it between his feet. "You played with Oscar, Lorenzo and Joe before I got here."

Shane came around the community center once or twice a week to mingle with the kids, to remind himself how much *he* had needed a role model at their age. "They're seventeen. No strategy. Now you...I have to use my brain as well as my reflexes when I go against you." Picking up his bottle of water on the sidelines, Shane took a few swallows.

"So, how's the marriage going?"

Shane took another swallow then set the bottle on the ground once more. "Subtle, Hobbs. Like an eighteen-wheeler. At least with Jana, she gives me a lead-in before she probes."

Adam shrugged. "Jana says you're as tight as a clam on this subject. What goes?"

Shane swiped the ball from Adam, aimed and sank it. "Nothing goes. Hope and I concentrate on Christopher."

Adam's voice floated over Shane's shoulder. "Twenty-four hours a day? After he's in bed?"

Shane shrugged, as if he hadn't spent more than one hour in his office, so distracted by Hope's presence in the house that he couldn't concentrate. "You know what it takes to be a parent. I'm learning how to handle him." Shane grimaced, remembering Thursday afternoon when he'd lost control of the situation. "And he's learning to handle me."

Adam grinned. "You mean get away with murder. The girls tried that with Jana but she was too smart to fall into that trap. We stood together and they realized they couldn't bamboozle either one of us." He paused. "Are you and Hope standing together?"

"We're trying." Shane retrieved the ball and jogged back. He gazed at the building that could use a good sandblasting, the teenagers shooting baskets at the other end of the lot, the few gathered on the asphalt watching the others. "Not many kids here today."

Adam didn't accept the change of subject. "You can't ignore your marriage."

Shane knew the lawyer in his friend wouldn't let him give up once he'd started something. "Ignore it? I'm trying to deal with it," Shane retorted. Adam only pried because he thought he could help, but the prying was irritating nonetheless.

"Have you ever considered how Davie's death affected you?" Adam asked, his eyes serious.

Silence fell between them. Finally, Shane broke it. "Of course I have. His death is the reason I quit being a cop, the reason my marriage fell apart!"

"More than that. It made you trust nobody but yourself. It was bad enough being a cop. You had to depend on your gut instinct, your training, your reflexes. But when it came to Davie, even those skills weren't enough."

"So what's your point?"

Adam shifted on his sneakers, but didn't back down. "You don't give of yourself easily. Your guard is up most of the time."

"I let it down once with Hope," Shane murmured, remembering that one night, when she'd held him, when she'd cried out his name in ecstasy....

"Are you giving her a chance now?"

Shane closed his mind to the pictures. "A chance to burn me again? I don't think so. I'm not stupid, Counselor."

"No, you're not. You're angry. About the way you had to grow up too fast, your mother's death, Davie, your divorce, Hope leaving you at the altar. What's that anger going to get you?"

Shane snapped the ball to his friend and Adam caught it reflexively. "Protection," he said. "Like a bulletproof vest. Don't worry about me, Adam. I know the score and so does Hope. We're aiming at peaceful coexistence. The fates willing, one day we'll have it." A voice asked, *Peaceful coexistence? Is that why you were ready to kiss her again?*

Shane shut out the voice. The longer he was around Hope, the less she would affect him.

Adam dribbled the ball in front of Shane. "Christmas is coming fast."

The comment seemed entirely out of context. "So?" He tensed his arms, ready to move in either direction.

"Maybe it'll bring the peace you want to find. Maybe it will bring even more."

Shane didn't get the chance to mull over Adam's words. His friend feinted to the left, then the right, and made a basket.

Sunday afternoon, the doorbell rang. Hope stood at the bottom of the stairs and heard the low vibrations of Shane's baritone as he put Christopher down for his nap. There was no point interrupting a ritual that was becoming precious to father and son.

Hope went to the door and opened it. A tall man stood there. She'd guess he was in his sixties from the wrinkles on his face and the silver in his dark hair, though his well-kept physique in an oxford shirt and jeans made him look younger.

"Hello there, young lady. You must be the gal who left the message."

"No, I'm—"

He didn't seem to hear her as he smiled sheepishly and kept going, restrained excitement buzzing all around him. "I was out of town on business. Just got back this morning. Sorry to bother you but there was no way I could wait till tomorrow to talk to Shane."

"Why don't you come in, Mr...."

"Just call me Harv." He took Hope's hand and pumped it up and down. "The message said Shane got a lead on Bernadette. I can't believe I'm finally going to set eyes on her after all these years. Just imagine. I don't know if Shane told you, but we were high school sweethearts."

It didn't seem to matter that Hope hadn't left the message for Harv. He probably thought she was Jana. He was so excited about what Shane had discovered, nothing else seemed to count.

"We went to school together in Houston. Who would've thought Shane would find her back East."

"You've been looking for a long time?"

"Actually, no. I just got up the gumption a few months ago and didn't know where to start. It was my fault we lost touch. I shipped out with the army. She wrote and I never wrote back. Damn, I was young and stupid and wild. Didn't want to be tied down, I thought."

"Well, Harv, I'm glad you're on your way to finding her."

"I'm unattached now. Been a widower seven years. I just hope she's free, too."

"I hope you find what you're looking for."

"If I find Bernadette, she's all I need."

"I know Shane's good at what he does. If anyone can find her, he can."

"Hello, Harv." Shane had come up behind Hope without her knowing it. "Let's go into my office."

Shane's tone dismissed her. He was going to have to accept the fact she wasn't easily dismissed. "It was good to meet you, Harv. I hope you find Bernadette." She went to the kitchen to start a pot roast for supper.

With the roast in the oven, Hope decided she had enough time to make an apple pie. She'd cut and peeled six cups of apples when Shane appeared in the kitchen doorway. She could tell he was thinking about something, about how to put it to her. He always got that little line on his forehead before he gave her bad news.

Although every nerve in her body was alive and shouting that he was in the same room, she calmly folded the pie shell in quarters and lifted it onto the top of the apples.

"You shouldn't have talked to Harv the way you did."

"Excuse me?"

AN IMPORTANT MESSAGE FROM THE EDITORS OF SILHOUETTE®

Dear Reader,

Because you've chosen to read one of our fine romance novels, we'd like to say "thank you"! And, as a **special** way to thank you, we've selected <u>four more</u> of the <u>books</u> you love so well, **and** a Porcelain Trinket Box to send you absolutely *FREE!*

Please enjoy them with our compliments...

Anne Canadeo Senior Editor,
Silhouette Romance

P.S. And <u>because</u> we value our customers, we've attached something extra inside ...

PEEL OFF SEAL AND PLACE INSIDE

HOW TO VALIDATE
YOUR
EDITOR'S FREE GIFT
"THANK YOU"

1. Peel off gift seal from front cover. Place it in space provided at right. This automatically entitles you to receive four free books and a beautiful Porcelain Trinket Box.

2. Send back this card and you'll get brand-new Silhouette Romance™ novels. These books have a cover price of $2.99 each, but they are yours to keep absolutely free.

3. There's no catch. You're under no obligation to buy anything. We charge nothing—ZERO—for your first shipment. And you don't have to make any minimum number of purchases—not even one!

4. The fact is thousands of readers enjoy receiving books by mail from the Silhouette Reader Service™ months before they're available in stores. They like the convenience of home delivery and they love our discount prices!

5. We hope that after receiving your free books you'll want to remain a subscriber. But the choice is yours—to continue or cancel, anytime at all! So why not take us up on our invitation, with no risk of any kind. You'll be glad you did!

6. Don't forget to detach your FREE BOOKMARK. And remember...just for validating your Editor's Free Gift Offer, we'll send you FIVE MORE gifts, *ABSOLUTELY FREE!*

YOURS FREE!

*This beautiful porcelain box is topped with a lovely bouquet of porcelain flowers, perfect for holding rings, pins or other precious trinkets — and is yours **absolutely free** when you accept our no risk offer!*

Shane kept his distance but jabbed his hands into his pockets. The gesture pulled the already snug jeans even snugger. "Harv is my client."

Trying to ignore the heat creeping up her cheeks, she said, "I know that."

"I give my clients facts. I don't raise their hopes needlessly."

"I don't understand. He said you had a lead. He said you knew Bernadette was back East...."

"Yes, I have a lead. That's all I have. You pumped him up, and now he thinks they're going to be reunited. Even if I do find her, what if she wants no part of him?"

"He was already pumped up when he rang the doorbell. All I did was—"

"Pump him up more. I run my business a certain way, Hope. Stay out of it, okay?"

She glared at him, thoroughly annoyed. "You can poke into my life and tell me not to take a job, but I can't go near your clients? Does that sound reasonable to you?"

Shane stood firm. "Yes. One has to do with our son's welfare, the other one doesn't."

She felt like turning that pie upside down on his stubborn head. "You know, Shane, your rules make sense to you, they don't make sense to me. Maybe you should give me a list, the parts of your life that are safe for me to talk about, the areas I should stay away from."

"Don't be ridiculous."

Slowly and deliberately, she said, "I don't think I'm the one being ridiculous."

Shane took his hands out of his pockets. "This is business. I give my clients factual information, and I don't feed their emotions. I find too many dead ends, and I will not give false hope."

"All I did was make conversation!"

His brown eyes were hard. "All you did was interfere. I had to bring Harv down to earth."

She turned back to the pie and opened the folded shell to give her hands something to do. "Fine. I'll stay away from your clients. When the doorbell rings, I won't answer it. Unless, of course, I have your permission. All right, Captain?"

"Hope..."

She didn't meet his gaze but crimped the edges of the pie shells, hurt edging out the annoyance she'd first felt.

The phone rang in Shane's office. She felt him hesitate, then move away to answer it. He was trying to keep her pigeonholed, to think of her only in association with their son. There was nothing she could do about that but live with it until Shane decided he wanted her in the rest of his life. She could be waiting a long time.

After reviewing his notes, Shane pushed his chair away from his desk. Harv's former sweetheart didn't drive and apparently didn't work. That made it harder to trace her. He'd found a record of her marriage to a Pennsylvania insurance salesman and the death certificate of that husband. But that's all he'd found. He had a contact on the East Coast checking real estate records. That's all he could do for now.

He heard the buzzer go off on the oven. A few minutes later, Hope went up the stairs, probably to get Christopher up from his nap. Shane sighed. He couldn't take a breath without thinking about her. She was complicating his life, stirring up feelings and hormones he'd thought were inactive, if not dead. They were active, all right, and very much alive. Confusing as hell. He'd almost kissed her again the other night, and it wouldn't have been any kind of test. Then he'd remembered what she'd done. He'd remembered that she'd walked out without telling him the truth.

But he still couldn't stay away from her. He definitely couldn't stay away from his son. He shut down the computer and went up to Christopher's bedroom.

Christopher had just awakened. His hair stood up in spikes as he rubbed his eyes. Hope sat on the edge of the bed, picking up books that lay on the floor beside it. Before Christopher fell asleep in the afternoons, she let him page through his favorites. Shane marveled at the way she could teach without words, the simple things she did to evoke Christopher's curiosity or instill a good habit. Her son didn't realize it, but Hope was doing everything she could to prepare him to read.

Finally, Christopher yawned and scrambled onto his mother's lap. "Where's your smile, Mommy?"

The little boy's question made Shane feel guilty. It was in Hope's nature to be bubbly and cheerful. Especially around her son, she smiled and laughed a lot. Right now, laughter seemed to be a world away and Shane suspected that had to do with their conversation.

He entered the room and didn't wait for Hope to answer. Conspiratorially, he stooped down to Christopher and whispered in his ear, "I think she left it down in the kitchen next to the pie she took out of the oven. Want me to go get it?"

Christopher nodded his head solemnly. "Uh-huh."

"All right. I'll be right back."

Shane galloped down the steps, went into the kitchen, took a quick glance around and picked up a pot holder. Then he climbed the steps and went into his son's room, holding the quilted square on his palm in front of Hope. "There it is, ma'am. All ready to put on. It must have fallen off when you opened the oven door." Shane hadn't spouted such silliness in a long time, not since he used to tease and play with Davie. He waited for the familiar stab of pain. It didn't come.

Hope didn't look quite so serious as she played along with his humorous scenario and said to Christopher, "Well, look at that smile. I didn't even realize it had fallen off."

When she switched her attention from her son to Shane, he saw the hurt lingering in her eyes. He never expected his criticism would bother her so much. Laying the pot holder gently on her lap, he said, "Whenever you're ready. I miss your smile, too."

Her gaze questioned him, searching for sincerity. She must have found it, because she pretended to lift something from the pot holder. She held it to her mouth, smoothing first over her top lip, then the bottom one. Her playful gesture was sensual without her knowing it.

Then she smiled and gave Christopher a hug. "Is that better?"

Her son nodded.

Shane wasn't sure it was better. Her smile packed a wallop, hitting him where he felt it most.

Wednesday evening, when Hope turned the end-table light down a notch in Jana's living room, Christopher didn't stir. Covering him with an afghan from the back of the sofa, she returned to Jana in her kitchen.

Shane's partner was pouring tea. "It's herbal so it won't keep you up tonight."

Hope sat on a chair and pulled it in to the table. "Thanks for inviting us for supper." Adam and Shane were attending a budget meeting at the community center. Jana had invited Hope, Shane and Christopher to dinner. After she'd put Matthew to bed, Christopher had conked out on the sofa.

"With the men at the meeting, I figured we'd have some time to talk. If you want to."

Seeing Jana and Adam together in their home, watching Shane's relationship with both of them, Hope knew she had nothing to be jealous about. She'd like to have Jana as a confidante but because of the woman's friendship with Shane, that might not be possible.

Hope pulled the cup of tea toward her. "What has Shane told you? About our marriage, I mean."

"That Christopher is his son, that you lied to him and walked out before the wedding. His words, not mine."

Hope picked up the cup, decided the tea was too hot to sip and put the cup back on the saucer. "I'm surprised you're friendly to me. You're Shane's friend."

Jana pulled out a chair and sat across from her. "I'm not making any judgments, Hope. I don't think most people hurt each other intentionally. We all do what we think is best at the time, and we all make mistakes."

"Adam doesn't think Shane should have married me, does he?"

"Adam wanted Shane to be sure about what he was doing."

"Shane's always sure about what he does," Hope murmured.

Jana gave her a wry smile. "You believe that tough-guy act?"

Hope sighed. "Sometimes I have no choice. Others . . ." She thought about that afternoon in her mother's garage when he suggested she keep the vanity, their incendiary kiss, his obvious love for their son. "Shane told me you're psychic. Sometimes I wish I were."

"And sometimes I wish I weren't. At times, words and sounds and impressions pop into my head about someone, about something, but I don't know if they're past, present or future. Usually I see a connection to the present."

Hope couldn't keep from asking, "What do you see about me and Shane?"

Jana took a sip of tea, then put her cup on the saucer. "I don't 'see' anything. I feel a strong connection between the two of you."

"Christopher."

Jana shook her head. "No. Much more than Christopher."

"I just can't make Shane understand why I didn't tell him...."

"If you love him, eventually he might understand. And if he doesn't, you'll have to make a decision that's right for you and your son."

Hope stiffened in her chair. "That sounds like a prediction."

Jana shook her head. "Nope. Experience. Adam and I had some rough patches, too. I thought he was still in love with his ex-wife."

Relaxing again, realizing Jana *could* be a friend, Hope said, "Tell me about you and Adam. Seeing you two together gives me hope. You seem so happy."

"We are." Jana told Hope how she met Adam, and how they fell in love.

She'd just finished relating how Adam had proposed when the phone rang. Excusing herself, she went to the living room to answer it. Adam and Shane returned by way of the back door as Jana reentered the kitchen. She looked troubled.

Adam crossed to her and kissed her on the forehead. "What's wrong?"

"I just received a phone call from a lawyer in Phoenix. When he couldn't reach Shane, he called me. The police department there gave him our number. He's looking for the daughter of a client who's seriously ill. He's checked all the databases and keeps hitting roadblocks. So he wants to know if we'll fly down and see if we can help. Before it's too late."

Adam asked, "Are you taking it?"

Jana glanced at Shane and he nodded. "Yes."

Shane asked his partner, "When do you want to leave?"

"Adam, what do you think?" Jana turned to her husband.

"I can work at home for a few days and take care of Matthew. If I have to go into the office, I'll call Mrs. Haynes."

"You're sure?"

Adam put his arm around his wife's shoulders. "I'm sure."

Hope's gaze found Shane's. "We'd better go home so you can pack."

"Is Christopher sleeping?"

"On the sofa."

"I'll get him."

After thanking Jana for supper, they left. In the car, Shane said, "I don't know when I'll be back."

This was the nature of Shane's work, she knew. It gave his schedule flexibility but also made immediate demands. "I know. Maybe I'll call Adam tomorrow and tell him I can keep Matthew if he needs to go to his office."

Shane gave her a quick, sideways glance. "Mrs. Haynes is like a grandmother to Matthew. He's used to her. But Adam might be glad to have a backup." After a pause, Shane said, "I don't like leaving you alone again so soon after the last time."

"It's all right. I understand."

Shane hesitated a moment. "I'll try to give you a number where you can reach me at all times. If there are any problems, don't hesitate to call Adam."

"And I have Eloise. Don't worry about us, Shane. Christopher and I are used to being on our own."

"You aren't on your own anymore." Shane's voice was husky.

His concern felt so good. It warmed her, made her heart feel lighter. Maybe time *would* lead to forgiveness and togetherness.

Shane packed while Hope put Christopher to bed. After she kissed her sleeping son good-night, she remembered clothes Shane might need and she went to get them from the laundry room.

Hands full, she pushed open the door to Shane's bedroom. The high, king-size four-poster bed was the focus of the room, though the armoire and nightstands were quality pieces, too. A cedar chest sat at the foot of the bed across from the fireplace and easy chair.

Shane tossed a few pairs of socks into the travel bag. "I've written down the number of the hotel. If I'm not there, the desk has a voice-mail system, so I'll get your message. If I can, I'll leave a number with the hotel where you can contact me."

Hope laid two knit shirts on the bed, remembering one cherished night there, remembering the love they'd shared. Shane looked up, saw her expression and his jaw tightened. His gaze passed over his clothes, the bed, Hope. The atmosphere between them hummed with all the tension that had surrounded them since she'd returned. She didn't know what to do or what to say.

Shane broke eye contact and resumed packing.

Hope took a few deep breaths. "I won't go Christmas shopping for Christopher until you get back."

He gave her the hint of a smile.

She stared at his large hands rearranging clothes, pushing over a shirt to fit in a can of shaving cream. His hands were so gentle, so caressing, so wonderfully tactile. Even his fingertip on her cheek could create excitement. Before she changed her mind, she said, "I'll miss you."

His smile faded. He threw the top of the bag over the bottom and zipped it. "Don't forget to put the security system on at night and when you're out."

"I won't."

"If you forget the code . . ."

They'd covered all this the first time he'd gone out of town. "I won't forget it, Shane. I gave the combination to Eloise."

She'd obviously made a mistake telling him she would miss him. Nothing she said brought them closer together. Time. She just had to wait. "I'll make breakfast before you leave tomorrow. Then Christopher can say goodbye."

Shane nodded.

Hope went to her room, closed the door and sat at the vanity Shane had encouraged her to keep. He did care. She just didn't know how much.

I'll miss you.

Hope's gentle voice echoed in Shane's head, and his body tightened. Each day became more of a battle, a battle against his emotions, a battle against his desire for her.

Staring out the window of the airplane into the blue of the sky and the white of the clouds, he didn't think he'd ever felt more weary in his life. Hope seemed to be softness and goodness, but he'd thought that once before and he'd gotten torn apart. Keeping his focus on Christopher was the only way to maneuver through this marriage...the only way.

He glanced over at Jana who had closed her eyes and was napping. How long had it been since he had a good night's sleep? No wonder he was so tired.

Shane closed his eyes, but didn't feel the calmness and peace of slumber. He saw Hope's face.

Hope's knitting needles worked in and out, in and out, as she tried to make progress on Shane's Christmas present. The sweater had become a symbol of the love she felt for him. The shade of hunter green would look wonderful with his tawny hair and deep brown eyes. She'd found a silk shirt the perfect color to blend with it.

When the phone rang, Hope reached for it eagerly.

"Hope, it's Shane."

He'd been gone two days and she'd done a lot of thinking. "Hi. How's it going?"

"I called to give you another number. We're staying in Grand Rapids now. Jana has a sense the woman we're looking for is about an hour and a half from here near a lake."

"So you don't have any idea when you'll be home?"

"I'm hoping in a couple of days. But I can't say for sure. I would have called last night, but we got back to the hotel too late."

Hope wouldn't have cared how late it was, but she was hesitant to say so. Shane always seemed to back away when she said she cared about him. Yet there was a quality in Shane's voice she didn't recognize, that urged her to ask, "Are you all right?"

"Fine. The mattress at the last hotel was as hard as concrete."

She smiled at his description. "Did you sleep at all?"

"Enough. How's Christopher?"

"Growing. I took him to the pediatrician Jana recommended. He's grown an inch and weighs three pounds more that he did before we left Wasco."

"Everything's all right, though? I mean, you just took him for a checkup."

"Everything's fine. I, uh, wanted to tell you I've come to a decision about the day-care job."

"Oh?" He sounded wary.

"I think you're right. It would be good for me to be home with Christopher. But, Shane, I would like to finish up my degree in early education so I can eventually teach. I could go to school part-time."

Shane was silent for a few moments. "You don't have much to finish up, do you?"

"No. Eloise said she'd keep Christopher while I'm in class."

"And you want to start course work in January?"

"I'd like to."

There was a long pause. "We can discuss it more when I get home. I have to go now, Hope. We're making an early start tomorrow."

Something urged her to say, "Take care of yourself."

"You, too."

Shane's goodbye was husky, and Hope wondered if he didn't miss her just a little.

The key missed the lock and Shane tried it again. This time it slipped in and the lock turned. As soon as he closed the door, he was aware of Hope's presence. Her blue gaze met his and she smiled, a smile that made his head throb along with other parts of his body.

Hope rose from the sofa. She wore a rose caftan that molded to her body as she moved toward him. Jeez! Just what he needed right now. He hadn't been able to get her out of his head the whole time he'd been gone. Even when he tried to come up with a Christmas list for Christopher.

"Welcome home."

He dropped his suitcase by the stairs. "I guess Christopher's in bed."

Her smiled flagged slightly. "About an hour ago. If I'd known you were coming home, I would have kept him up. Was your trip successful?"

He hadn't called because they'd barely had time to catch the flight out tonight instead of waiting until morning. He'd felt this draw to get back to L.A., to Christopher and Hope, that he'd never felt before. "Thanks to Jana, it was. She's incredible. The woman we found flew back to Phoenix to see her father, and we flew home."

Hope stepped closer to him, and he could smell the bubble bath she used. The scent often lingered in her bathroom after she'd gone to bed. Once in a while when he passed it to gaze at his sleeping son, he'd stop and take in the flowery smell. It was stupid, really. Thank God he had his own bathroom off his bedroom. That's all he would need—to find Hope naked some morning...or night...or anytime in between.

"Shane?"

Her soft voice sounded far away. But she was very close, too close. He needed some air. "I've been cooped up in planes and hotel rooms too long. I'm going out for a run."

"Now?"

"Yes, now. You don't have to wait up." He lifted his suitcase and took it up to his room.

Hope didn't know what she expected with Shane's homecoming, but she'd hoped for more than she'd gotten. On top of Shane's remoteness, she sensed something was different...wrong. A huskiness in his voice, a fatigue in his tone and demeanor she'd never heard or seen before. What he needed was a good meal and a massage to loosen the knots from traveling. Oh, would she like to give him a massage!

Hope Walker, behave yourself.

She sighed. Unfortunately, she would behave. She had no choice.

Hope had just put the finishing touches on a tray of cheese and crackers when she heard Shane return. She hurried to the living room before he could go upstairs. What she saw made her run to him. "Shane, what's wrong?"

Chapter Six

Bent over, with his hands on his knees, Shane's face was flushed, his breathing ragged. When Hope took hold of his shoulder, it burned her hand. Had he gotten overheated while running?

She slipped her arm around his waist. "Let me help you."

He started for the sofa. "I don't need help." He almost made it before he stumbled.

Ignoring his protest, she curled her arm around his waist. "You're scaring me, Shane. Let me help you."

His gaze burned into her, but he nodded. "All right."

At the sofa, he sank onto the cushions and laid his head against the back. She sat next to him and felt his forehead. He was sweating but there was a burning heat underneath that hadn't developed from his run. Taking his wrist between her fingers, she took his pulse.

"What are you doing?"

"I've had emergency training. Just keep quiet for a minute." His pulse was strong but much too fast. "What's going on, Shane?"

He shook his head, then looked as if he regretted the motion. "I've felt so damn tired the last few days."

"Has your throat been scratchy?"

He glanced at her sideways. "How did you know?"

"The tone of your voice has been different. Don't move," she commanded. "I'm going to get the thermometer."

He straightened, then held his head. "I don't need—"

"I'm trying to find out what you need. *I* need to find out exactly what condition you're in. Now stay put or I won't pick you up when you fall on the floor." Her threat was empty, and they both knew it. But Shane didn't argue. It was probably the picture of him falling on the floor that kept him still. He hated to appear weak in front of anyone.

She raced upstairs and found the thermometer she kept in her bureau drawer. She had a sixth sense where Christopher was concerned. She could tell how high his fever was just by touching him. With Shane . . . She suspected it was higher than even he imagined. It had to be to put him in this condition.

Downstairs, she slipped the thermometer into Shane's mouth. Her fingers touched his lips and the heat in his gaze came from more than the fever. Shaken, but knowing she'd have to get past this strain between them to take care of him, she said, "I'm going to boil water for tea and get you a glass of orange juice. If that fever is as high as I think it is, you need to get liquids into you."

"I hate tea."

"Coffee's out because of the caffeine. The tea is herbal. It will help settle your stomach."

He took the thermometer out of his mouth. "How do you know my stomach needs settling?"

"You're looking at the cheese and crackers as if they're going to hop up and bite you. The Shane I know can eat anytime, anyplace, anywhere." She took the thermometer from him and stuck it back in his mouth. "Don't talk till I come back."

He gave her a defiant glare.

Rolling her eyes, she went to the kitchen, suspecting he was going to be one recalcitrant patient, worse than her son when he was sick. Unfortunately, she couldn't give Shane a coloring book and crayons to entertain himself. He'd always been a man on the move, but he was probably going to feel worse before he felt better.

When she returned to the living room, his eyes were glassy. Slipping the thermometer from his mouth, she read it—103 degrees. He took it from her and blinked so he could focus. "That can't be right."

She laid it on the coffee table. "You're sick, Shane. You probably have a virus that has to run its course. But if we don't get this fever down by tomorrow, we should call the doctor."

"I don't need a doctor," he growled.

"Then cooperate with me."

"And what's that supposed to mean?"

She stood and planted her hands on her hips. "Don't fight with me. Do what I tell you to do."

He gave her a disgruntled grimace. "All I need is a good night's sleep." Edging to the rim of the couch, he tried to stand and slumped back down.

"You need a good night's sleep, but you need fluids and aspirin and maybe a sponge bath, too."

That suggestion brought his eyes to hers. "Forget it."

"At least let me help you get upstairs."

After a silence, he said with resignation, "All right. The room spins every time I move."

Progress. Maybe.

Shane pushed up, levering himself on the arm of the sofa. Hope's arm circled his waist, and she took his weight. He was hot, and damp, and so extremely male. She loved being this close to him; she loved helping him. He hated it.

"Are you ready?" she asked gently. She felt his nod and they moved toward the stairs.

Shane was a tall man, lean, but pure muscle. In the up-stairs hall, she stopped and propped him against the wall for a moment.

"Are you okay?" he murmured.

Catching her breath, she said, "I'm fine. Just a little far-ther."

When Shane collapsed on his bed, Hope breathed a sigh of relief...until she realized he was shivering. "Do you have a pair of pajamas?"

He dropped his head into his hands. "Never wear them."

Searching in his dresser drawer, she found a pair of flan-nel jogging shorts and a T-shirt.

"Hope, I'm fine."

"You can't crawl into bed in clothes that are sweaty from running. Do you want to get better or catch pneumonia?"

"You're worse than a nurse," he grumbled as he tugged his shirt over his head. "Throw me the clothes."

"I'll go get the tea and orange juice." She laid the clothes beside him on the bed.

A short time later, the glassware on the tray jiggled as Hope carried it into Shane's room. He was lying in bed, the covers pulled over him, his eyes closed. She knew he needed to rest, but first he needed to get the aspirin and fluids down. She placed the tray on the nightstand and sat down on the bed next to him.

Opening his eyes, he saw her and the tray. "Hope..."

"If you don't listen, you'll be setting a bad example for Christopher."

"That's blackmail."

"That's the truth."

"He's not even awake."

"If you'd expend less energy arguing with me and more doing what you're told, you'd be sleeping by now."

"I never realized how stubborn you can be," he mut-tered.

She raised her eyebrows. "Which do you want first? Juice, water or tea?"

When he reached for the glass of water, his hand shook. She handed it to him with the aspirin. "Are you cold?"

He nodded. "Even the covers aren't helping."

"Will you let me sponge you down?"

"No way, lady," he snapped as he gulped down the aspirin and grimaced.

"Does that hurt?"

"I'll survive."

"Life is about more than surviving, Shane. Work on that cup of tea. I'll be right back."

"Stubborn and bossy, too," he mumbled, but did as he was told.

She'd always loved the idea of a fireplace in the bedroom. Tonight, a fire would help break Shane's fever. She'd spotted kindling and logs in the shed outside. Loading the carrier she found by the fireplace downstairs, she wondered just how bossy and stubborn Shane would let her be. She'd rather crawl in beside him and warm him with her body, but if he wouldn't agree to a sponge bath, she doubted he'd agree to that.

He was huddled under the covers again when she brought the wood into his bedroom. His eyes were closed. She laid the fire and had just touched it with a match when he opened them.

"This should help you get warm. If it doesn't, I'll get you another blanket."

"Hope, you don't have to do this."

Standing at the foot of the bed, she rested her hand on one of the posts. "We're married, Shane. Caring for each other is part of that, at least for me. That's one of my rules to go with all the others you made up." She nodded toward the tea. "Try to get the rest of that down." Then she turned and left the room.

* * *

After picking up a novel she'd started one night when she couldn't get to sleep, Hope checked on Christopher, then returned to Shane. His room had warmed up and he looked as if he'd fallen asleep.

The armchair in the sitting area of the room was heavy, but she managed to nudge it with her knee away from the fireplace and closer to the bed. Then she turned off the lights and settled into it, ready to keep her vigil. She dozed, waking when she heard Shane tossing and turning. Hurrying to his side, she felt his forehead. It still burned her hand. Stoking the fire, she resettled in her chair and nodded off.

A few hours had passed when she awakened again. In the shadows, she sat beside Shane and felt his forehead. Beads of perspiration told her the high fever had broken. Crossing to the dresser, she took out another T-shirt and pair of shorts, then went to the kitchen and poured apple juice. It wouldn't burn like the orange juice when it went down his throat.

Beside Shane once again, she shook him awake gently then held the glass out to him with two more aspirin.

He didn't argue and managed to drink half the juice. That was a good sign. But they had another hurdle to cross.

"You can't sleep in those clothes. You'll get more chilled."

Even in the dark with only the embers of the fire casting shadows around the room, she could feel Shane's gaze on her. He tried to sit up straighter, but dropped his head back on the pillow. "Forget it."

"C'mon. I'll help you."

He tried to sit up again. Hope was quick and tugged his shirt up his arms and over his head. Her fingers grazed his ribs. She wished she could lay her cheek against his chest rather than hand him his shirt. Unfolding the shirt to make it easier for him to put on, she gave it to him. Their hands touched and she saw him wince. "I know, your skin hurts when you have this kind of fever."

He let the comment stand. "I can take care of my shorts."

She let him try, but his strength seemed to give out when he'd pushed them to his knees. He swore.

"Shane, it's dark. I'm certainly not going to see anything, if that's what you're worried about."

"I'm not worried about anything. Go ahead. Drag them off." She tried to slip the shorts off without flipping back the sheet. That wasn't too hard. But she couldn't help him put the fresh ones on that way. Ignoring his grunt of disapproval, she turned back the sheet and started his shorts up his legs, pretending not to look at anything else. Pretending, because she knew what Shane looked like. His long legs, powerful thighs, and . . .

She took a deep breath.

He sat up, and his hands closed over hers. She went still, her gaze finding his face in the dimmest of light. "This is too dangerous," he said, his voice husky. "Go back to your room."

Dangerous for him, or dangerous for her?

He went on in a raspy voice, "Every time you breathe, I can see that damn drape outline your breasts. No wonder I'm sweating. Go back to your room, Hope. We'll both sleep better."

Had he been watching her when she thought he was sleeping? She ignored his warning. "Move over to the other side of the bed where the sheets are dry. The next time you wake up, I want to take your temperature. If it's down, I'll go back to my room. For now, I'm staying." She tilted her head. "Unless you want to throw me out." They both knew he was in no shape to do that.

"You're going to get a stiff neck in that chair."

"It's really not bad."

"Hope . . ."

"Right now, Shane, I'm a lot stronger than you are."

"You want to test it?" he growled.

Her heart raced. Even in the condition he was in, if she challenged him, she had no doubt he'd meet it. "No." Handing him the glass of water, she ordered, "Drink."

He took the glass and managed to get most of the liquid down. Then he moved over to the other side of the bed and lay back on the pillow. Finally, his eyes closed. Hope breathed a sigh of relief and went downstairs to refill the water glass.

When she stepped back into the room, Shane was muttering in his sleep. As she added kindling, and stoked the almost burnt-out fire back to life, Shane's muttering became louder, more intelligible.

"No, no, not Davie. Oh my God, nooo..." He tossed first to the left, then to the right.

Hope hurried to him. He'd turned away from her, and not knowing what else to do, she gently rubbed the middle of his back. He stopped moving restlessly, and his muscles seemed to relax. She kept rubbing. She didn't know how long she soothed, how long she rubbed his spine, the broad span between his shoulders. After he'd been quiet for some time, she stopped.

His blond-brown hair curled around his ear and lay at the nape of his neck. She couldn't help wanting to touch it. Brushing it away from his ear, she put a tender kiss on his cheek. Then she went back to her chair to continue her vigil.

The sun was barely creeping over the window ledge when she awoke. She stretched and yawned, then sat up and looked over at Shane. To her surprise, he was sitting on the edge of the bed. "Going somewhere?"

"Yes. To the bathroom. My fever must be down because the room's standing still."

She didn't believe him, but approached him and touched her hand to his forehead. "Not quite as bad. But I want to take your temperature anyway to make sure."

0

KAREN ROSE SMITH 117

He pushed himself off the bed and took hold of the nightstand.

"Shane..."

"I'm fine," he muttered as he used the wall to make his way to the bathroom. She held her breath until he re-emerged, still on his feet. Just barely. When he got to the bed, he stretched out, his breathing labored.

"Was it really worth the effort to do that by yourself?"

He closed his eyes. "Yes."

She sighed and reached for the thermometer. When she touched it to his lips, he opened his eyes. They bored into her, and she wondered what he was thinking.

His temperature was down to 101 degrees. She handed him aspirin and the glass of water. After he swallowed the pills, he said, "Go to your room and get some sleep."

"Only if you promise to call if you need me."

"I'll call."

She was sure he wouldn't, but she realized that her presence could keep him from resting. With nurselike precision, she straightened his covers. "You try to sleep, too."

He nodded.

She left his door open, hoping she'd hear him if he got out of his bed. When she crawled into hers, she wondered if he'd resent her for the care she'd given him, for seeing him weaker than he wanted to be. But it didn't matter if he did because she'd do it all again. She loved him.

Shane's head throbbed when he woke up, but not nearly as badly as it had the night before. He'd seen the worry in Hope's eyes. He'd been worried himself. He never got sick!

Suddenly, he remembered the nightmare. An old one. More than the nightmare, he remembered Hope's hand on his back. He'd almost shrugged her away but it had felt so good...calming. He'd almost stopped breathing when she'd brushed the hair from his neck, when she'd kissed him. Had that been a dream? His overactive libido working even in his sleep? He had watched her resting in that chair and, as bad as he'd felt, had become aroused by it.

She'd fought to take care of him last night. Why? Did he dare believe she really cared? That she hadn't come back into his life for convenience or to make her life easier? Why hadn't she fought like that four years ago? Why hadn't she stood her ground and told him she was pregnant? If she'd loved him, she would have. If she'd loved him . . .

Damn! He was getting sucked in all over again because of a little kindness. He'd better get his guard back up and fast. He hated feeling weak; he hated feeling defenseless. Must be the flu.

The door to his room opened and Hope came in carrying a tray. Christopher was right behind her but waited at the threshold. She smiled at Shane. "He wanted to make sure for himself that you're all right."

Shane mustered up the best smile he could. "I'm getting better. But you'd better stay clear until I can come downstairs. I don't want you getting sick."

His son's brown eyes got wider. "Mommy says Thanksgivin's soon. You gonna be okay then?"

Thanksgiving was ten days away. "I'm sure I'll be fine by then."

Hope said, "Play in your room for a few minutes till I take your dad's temperature."

"Okay." Christopher scampered off.

"He's a good kid."

"And a better patient than you are." She held out the thermometer to him. "Here. You can have breakfast after I take your temperature."

This time he didn't argue with her. The scrambled eggs looked light enough to float down his throat, and his stomach rumbled.

She laughed. "Good. You have an appetite."

He had an appetite for more than her food.

Shane checked the thermometer before he gave it to her. "It's only 99. I'm better already. Good thing, too. I have calls to make, paperwork to go through...."

"Shane Walker, don't you even think about stepping out of this room, let alone going into your office. If you don't behave today, I'll call Adam."

Shane couldn't suppress his smile. "And just what do you think Adam's going to do?"

"Sit on you if he has to. There's no reason you can't stay in bed and relax today. I called Jana and she said she'll be in, and can handle any emergencies that come up."

"You had no right to—"

"Tell her that her partner is a little under the weather? I don't need rights to do that. A secretary would have done the same thing."

Hope was right. He didn't know why he was being so argumentative. Maybe because she was invading every area of his life, and he felt crowded. After a lengthy pause, he asked, "Truce?"

She smiled. "Does that mean I don't have to call Adam?"

"It means I appreciate everything you did for me last night."

Today, Hope wore jeans and a T-shirt that were every bit as appealing as the caftan that had swirled around her last night. Her smile slipping away, she came closer. "You had a nightmare last night. Do you remember it?"

Shane blanked out the pictures that were ready to flood his head. "Yes. It's the same one I always have. The car in flames, Mary Beth screaming..."

"It might help if you talked about it."

Shane hadn't talked about it to very many people. Even with Hope and her mother, then Adam and Jana, he'd merely given the briefest details. "There isn't anything to talk about. Davie died and it was my fault."

"Shane, you can't still believe that."

"The bomb was in my car, meant for me. It was my fault. If that had been Christopher, you'd blame me, too."

She sat on the bed next to him and covered his hand with hers. "Are you so sure of that? Your loss was as great as Mary Beth's. I can see how much you love Christopher. I can imagine how much you loved Davie. Some thug killed your son. You have to realize that you weren't to blame, or you'll never have any peace."

The pain in Shane's chest became so great, his throat tightened painfully. Hope's hand on his was like a lifeline, a way out of the pain. He studied their hands. She couldn't be his lifeline. He couldn't need her that much. If he did, and she left again...

Hope looked at him with such compassion, he wanted to pull her down beside him on the bed, kiss her rosy lips, stroke her soft skin, breathe in every part of her. His pulse thudded and so did his head, bringing him back to reality with a jolt.

He reached for the tray she'd set at the foot of the bed. "I'd better get started on the eggs. If you have things to do downstairs, don't worry about me. I'll remember to take more aspirin in a few hours." Knowing he sounded gruff, he settled the tray on his lap.

Hope stood. "I'll check back in a little while to see if you need anything. But I won't bother you if you're resting."

When she left his room, he wanted to call her back. But he didn't know what he'd say if he did, so he kept silent.

The following evening, Hope reached for Christopher's block at the same time as Shane. Their fingers brushed and the heat between them had nothing to do with the blaze in the living room fireplace. Shane's gaze had been on her all evening, as if he was trying to figure something out. They both chose different blocks to add to their son's architectural masterpiece.

When Shane had awakened this morning, his fever had disappeared. He'd worked with Jana in the office most of the day. By supper, he'd looked tired, but his complexion had the ruddy color of renewed health.

Suddenly, Christopher's building collapsed on the coffee table. The three-year-old just giggled. "Do it again."

Hope glanced at her watch. "Nope. It's time for bed."

Glancing first at Shane and then at his mother, he accepted her verdict. "Can Daddy read *two* stories tonight?"

Christopher had missed Shane while he was gone and the two days he'd been sick. Hope waited for Shane to answer.

"Help me gather up the blocks, then we'll pick out two books."

A smile lit Hope's heart. Shane was getting good at handling Christopher.

Hope enjoyed the ritual of putting their son to bed. It was the time when she felt closest to Shane. Tonight, while he was reading to Christopher nestled in his lap, she felt his searching gaze on her.

After they'd tucked in their son, Hope preceded Shane down the stairs, wondering what was coming. Sitting on the sofa, she waited.

Shane crossed to the fireplace and stared into the leaping fire. Finally, he turned and looked at her. She felt she could go up in flames as easily as the extra kindling on the hearth. "I've been thinking about what you said, about going back to school. If that's what you want to do, it's all right with me. Do you want me to pay for it, or will you use the proceeds from the sale of your mother's property in Arizona?"

His question took her aback. "I'd like to save that money for Christopher's education."

"From what you've said, it'll probably be a drop in the bucket. Besides, he won't need that money. I'll be paying for his education."

"Both of us have the responsibility for his education. Both of us should be working together for all of our needs."

"Because California's a community property state?" His brown eyes were unreadable.

"I don't understand what you mean."

"What's mine is yours and what's yours is mine?"

She hadn't really thought about all that. "Yes, I guess. Though the land in Arizona might not sell for a while."

"It could be a very long while," Shane agreed, still giving nothing away.

"I don't know what you're getting at, Shane. It's a little late for a prenuptial agreement. I'm surprised you didn't have Adam draw one up before the wedding." She couldn't keep the hurt from her voice. Standing so she'd feel as if she was on more equal footing, she tried to keep her voice calm. "I have a job at the day-care center if I want it, but you don't want me to work while Christopher's at home. I'd like to go back to school, yet you're going to resent paying for it. Am I right?"

Shane mowed his hand through his hair, a sure sign of frustration. "No, I won't resent paying for it, not if we're working toward the same goal of building a life together."

What in heaven's name did he think she was trying to do if not build a life with him? The suspicion he'd voiced before hit her with renewed force. "Do you still think I married you for security?"

He came closer to her, almost within touching distance. She could smell the trace of after-shave he'd used that morning, see the shadow line of his beard and feel the tension in his body as all that was past, present and maybe future vibrated between them.

His eyes darkened as he said, "I think you were tired of trying to make ends meet. Tired of working and trying to give Christopher attention at the same time. Tired of not capturing your dream. Marrying me solved all your problems."

The spark of anger inside her flared. She was tired of his suspicions, tired of feeling as if she was guilty of some terrible wrong. "Solved them? Let me tell you, Shane Walker, my 'problems,' as you put it, were a cinch compared to living with your distrust. Maybe this Christmas you should ask for a heart to replace that block of stone in your chest." As soon as she said it, she knew she'd gone too far.

Shane reached for her and crushed her against him. "Stone? You think any part of me is made of stone? Let's see what you think after this."

His mouth covered hers as his arms tightened her against him. The hardness she felt was hot and pulsing with life. Not stone...but male and heat and desire. His embrace and his kiss demanded she respond. Should she meet his demand or would she regret it if she did?

Chapter Seven

Shane's lips opened on hers, his tongue broke the seam of her lips and thrust inside. The strength of his passion melted doubts, the fervor of his desire engulfed her. She'd waited so long for him to hold her in his arms. Reveling in being where she most wanted to be, she curved her arms around his neck and laced her fingers in his hair. It was longer than she'd ever known it to be. She loved its vitality, its thickness, the slide of it through her fingers.

His tongue stroked hers, dashed against the roof of her mouth as if he couldn't taste her fast enough. Angling his head, his hands passed up and down her back. She wanted him as much as he wanted her. The fullness in his jeans tempted her, urging her to become bolder. While she stroked his jaw with one hand, she rubbed her breasts against his chest. His groan vibrated through her.

He broke their kiss, and she protested. But he'd only stopped to edge his fingers under her sweater and yank it over her head. His gaze went directly to her breasts and their rosy peaks showing through the lace cups. Quicker than she could blink, he unhooked her bra and held one rough palm to each breast. She loved the feel of his calluses on her skin. On the sensitive skin of her breasts, the stimulation was almost more than she could stand. She closed her eyes to absorb the wonder of his touch. Suddenly, she felt the wet, rough texture of his tongue sliding against her nipple, and she moaned. When he did it again, her knees buckled. He held her as they slid to the floor.

Palming her breasts, he kissed her hard, again and again and again. Hope couldn't keep her world right side up. But she was aroused enough to know she wanted his skin against hers, his body filling hers. She reached for the buttons on his shirt, trying to concentrate on slipping one after the other out of their holes. After she managed the last button, she slid her hand across his chest.

Shane laid her back on the floor and unsnapped her jeans. She reached for his. "I want you, Shane. It's been so long'..."

Her voice penetrated the haze. For the first time since he'd kissed her, he stilled and gazed into her eyes. She saw anguish there and didn't know why. "What's wrong?"

He swore viciously and looked away. "This is wrong."

"We're married, Shane."

His voice was gravelly. "Hope, the way things are between us . . . what happens if we have sex and regret it?"

She sat up, conscious of her nudity, but more concerned with what Shane was thinking. "You seem sure that would happen."

He stared into her eyes. "When I make love with you, Hope, I don't want to have doubts. I don't want to wonder if you told me about our son so I could take care of you both. I don't want to wonder if you're pretending something you don't feel."

He was as vulnerable as she was, maybe more so because he was so good at hiding it. "And what about you, Shane?

How am I supposed to know what you feel if you don't tell me?''

"I'm telling you now."

"What do you feel?"

For a moment, she thought he wouldn't respond, that he would button his shirt and walk away. Instead, he ran his hand across his forehead, then answered her. "I want you, Hope. Plain and simple. My body and my mind remember what we shared. But I won't be that blind again. I need to be sure we're going to make it before I give you more than my body."

"I can't separate my mind from my body," she said softly. "I loved you then and I love you now."

Anger creased his forehead and vibrated in his words. "If you'd loved me, you wouldn't have left. My father left. In her way, my mother left. That's not love. Maybe you'd better decide what love means to you. Because to me it means sticking together no matter what."

"I promised I'd stay when I married you."

He shook his head. "Promises can be broken. That adage is true that actions speak louder than words. We haven't been together long enough for me to trust in your promises this time."

Her eyes filled with tears, but she also felt a glimmer of hope. He'd been honest with her. He'd unlocked his feelings and let her see his vulnerability. Because of that, she believed they could have a good marriage. She'd prove to him he could trust her or she'd die trying.

Avoiding his gaze, she reached for her bra. Shane turned away and snapped his jeans. The awkwardness between them couldn't get any worse. She slipped her sweater on and ran her fingers through her hair. Sensing Shane had closed himself off again and further discussion about their marriage wouldn't solve anything, she searched for something tangible to talk to him about, to keep the connection between them.

"Thanksgiving is coming up soon. What would you like to do?"

Slowly, he buttoned his shirt. "Did you have something in mind?"

"I'd like to ask Aunt El to dinner, of course. Do you think Adam and Jana would like to join us?"

"Adam is flying Jana's mother in for the holidays."

"They could all come here," she suggested.

Shane studied her as if she were a puzzle he couldn't quite put together. "You sure you want to take on a dinner that size?"

"Thanksgiving is about family and extended families. I think we'd all enjoy it."

"Do you want me to ask Adam and Jana?"

"No, I'll do it. And maybe next week we could go Christmas shopping for Christopher?"

"We did say we'd do that."

He wasn't pushing her away, even after sharing what he had. That gave her so much hope her heart almost flipped over in her chest. "I'm going to prove to you that you can trust me, Shane. I'm going to prove I love you."

He met her eyes and cocked his head.

She felt more naked than she had a few minutes ago when her clothes had lain in disarray on the floor.

His voice was gentle as he said, "We'll have a large Thanksgiving dinner if that's what you want, and we'll go Christmas shopping together. But you and I both know things won't change overnight."

She wasn't that naive. But she was filled with more hope than even she thought possible. Christmas was a time for wishes to come true, and she'd always believed in Christmas magic. Maybe she could show Shane it was time for him to believe, too.

As Shane walked by shelves of toys the day after Thanksgiving, he actually felt happy. He had hardly remembered the feeling of lightness, the wonder of laughter, the simple joy of smiling. Hope had made Thanksgiving Day a holiday to remember. He was grateful to her for that, and a lot more—giving him a chance to get to know his son, championing their relationship, taking care of him when he was sick. It had been a long time since anyone had taken care of him. He'd hated the feeling of powerlessness at the time, but...

In his mind's eye, he could see her sitting by his bed in the light of the fire.

He needed a way to thank her. And yesterday Eloise had reminded him about Hope's birthday on December nineteenth. In a quiet moment, he and her aunt had discussed how difficult the holidays would be for Hope this year without her mother. That's when the idea had hit. A surprise party for Hope. Christopher would love it, too, though Shane knew better than to tell him about it before the day of the party.

Hope walked down the aisle of the toy store beside Shane. Remote-control cars lined the shelves. Shane picked up the demonstrator model and set it on the floor. He pushed a button and it ran over Hope's toe.

He grinned. "Sorry."

Hope teased, "Do you want that for Christopher or yourself?"

He looked as sheepish as a five-year-old. "Maybe we should get two. Then we could race them."

His crooked smile melted her. They were almost through the toy store and their cart was stocked full of books, games, a stuffed panda bear, a backhoe practically as big as Christopher, a computer that could help a child learn to read, a baseball mitt, and a variety of stocking stuffers.

"Maybe you should ask Santa for one."

Shane's gaze was hot on hers. "I've got a few things on my list that are a cut above remote-control cars."

"A Ferrari?" she asked.

"How about an old-fashioned Christmas with all the trimmings?"

"That would be my wish, too," she said softly.

The heat between them sizzled as Shane came toward her. He stopped directly in front of her. If he leaned forward, their bodies would touch. "You made yesterday special. I wanted to thank you."

Her light jacket seemed heavier, the temperature in the store higher. "No thanks are necessary."

"You did most of the work. Jana's mother couldn't stop raving about your pumpkin pies."

"She was being polite."

"Yeah, so were Adam and I when we almost ate a whole one ourselves."

Heat crawled up her cheeks. Thanksgiving Day had gone well. There had been laughter and hugs and wishes on the wishbone. "I'm glad you enjoyed it. Jana's mom and Aunt El got along great. They're going to have lunch together next week. Did you notice how good Christopher was with Matthew?"

Shane's eyes narrowed and he leaned away.

"I just mean I think he misses being with other children. I'd like to look around for a preschool a few hours a week if you don't mind."

Shane picked up the toy car at her feet and returned it to the display. "In Wasco, I guess you put him in the same day-care center where you worked."

"It was an ideal situation. I could be around him and work at the same time."

His eyebrows hiked up. "Ideal?"

"You know what I mean, Shane. At least when I went to work, I didn't have to leave him with a stranger. I took him with me, and I knew the women who were taking care of him."

"And you think he misses being with other kids?" In a
lower voice, almost to himself, he added, "Sometimes kids
aren't good for one another."

She knew he was thinking of the gangs of kids who got
into trouble. "Christopher is three. He needs other children to learn how to share, to learn how to make friends, to
learn how to win and lose at games."

Shane's stance became more relaxed. "You always think
about what's best for him, don't you?"

"I hope so."

Shane added one of the remote-control cars to the cart.
"All right. Tell me the truth. Did I go overboard here?"

Hope put her finger thoughtfully to her chin and carefully sorted through the merchandise. "I think you've made
good choices. If we can get out of the store without adding
anything else, you did just fine." The golden lights in
Shane's eyes warmed Hope and encouraged her. Thanksgiving *and* tonight had brought them closer together.

As Shane pushed the cart into the aisle, he said, "I forgot to tell you. I found Harv's high school sweetheart."

"You did? Where?"

"The real estate records led us to her. She'd bought a
cottage at Nags Head after her husband died. No telephone. Not much contact with anyone. But Harv flew out
before Thanksgiving. He called this morning to tell me he
was bringing her back with him."

"What do you think will happen?"

"That's anybody's guess. They both might have changed
a lot in all these years."

"Or maybe not so much."

Shane's sideways glance told her he was thinking about
the two of them, not Harv and his sweetheart. She and
Shane hadn't changed, not in the ways that mattered. Now
all she had to do was convince him.

* * *

Sunday morning after breakfast, Hope carefully lifted an ornament from the carton and examined it. The tiny wooden rocking horse barely covered her palm.

Shane turned from the tree where he'd attached strings of lights. "That should do it."

"C'n we put stuff on?" Christopher asked.

"Sure can." Shane peeked over Hope's shoulder. "That looks like an old one."

The scent of Shane's after-shave teased her. His long, tall body behind her sent awareness through her. "Most of them are. Christopher and I had started our own collection, but these are Mom's." She handed the rocking horse to her son. "Hang it wherever you'd like."

"Whatever you're baking smells good," Shane commented, his breath fanning her ear.

"Cranberry bread," she managed to say.

He reached around her and took an ornament from the box. When he hung it on the tree, she watched the play of muscles under his T-shirt. Trying to concentrate on decorating for Christmas rather than on Shane's attributes, she reached for a felt-wrapped item. "Look what I found, Christopher." She unfolded the green fabric. "It's our Christmas angel."

"Lemme see."

Hope held up the gold metallic angel with the slim chimes dangling from her gown.

"Where are we gonna put her?"

"I think the back porch might be best."

"So she c'n see Santa coming," Christopher added.

"Santa?" Shane asked with a grin.

"Uh-huh. We hang her outside and whenever Santa is in the area, she chimes," Hope answered.

Shane's grin broadened. "I see. I'll find a hammer and nail and we'll see if we can find the right spot."

Hope and Christopher waited for Shane on the back porch while he found what he needed in the shed.

On the porch, he tapped a nail into the edge of the eave and held out his hand for the angel. Hope gave the ornament to him, and Shane slipped the ring onto the nail.

"All set. Just waiting for some Christmas magic." He leaned close to Hope and whispered in her ear, "Or the wind."

She swatted his shoulder playfully.

Shane tweaked the tip of her nose. "You let me know when you hear Santa. I'd like to get a glimpse of him."

"Me, too," Christopher agreed.

Hope planted her hands on her hips. "You don't have to see him to know he's around. When you hear the Christmas angel, you only have to believe."

The timer went off in the kitchen. "Now that's a sound I believe in," Shane remarked. "Something good is coming out of the oven. C'mon, sport. Let's get back to decorating that tree while your mom gets the cranberry bread."

Shane took his son's hand and led him inside.

Hope wanted Shane to believe in the Christmas angel because everyone deserved a touch of magic in his life—especially Shane. She remembered the smile on his face as he tweaked her nose. They were growing closer. Someday soon he'd trust her again and then their marriage could really begin.

On the nineteenth of December, the trays of sandwiches, cheeses and vegetables filled the bottom shelves of Shane's refrigerator. He put two liters of soda on the top shelf. He and Christopher had just made a trip to the grocery store to pick up everything.

"Balloons now?"

Once Shane had told his son they were going to decorate with balloons for his mom's birthday, Christopher had thought of nothing else. "Okay, buddy. I'll blow them up, you can help put them where they look good."

The doorbell rang. Shane frowned. He'd canceled his appointments for the afternoon. Fortunately, Jana had convinced Hope to go shopping. Eloise wasn't due with the cake until five.

Pushing the pack of balloons in front of his son, Shane said, "Pick out the colors you like and we'll start with them."

Christopher grinned and reached for a red one.

As Shane walked through the living room, the scent of pine, the nativity set on the corner table, the pillar candles, boughs and shiny balls on the mantel made him smile. Hope sure had a knack for decorating. She had a knack for a lot of things—making his house feel like a home among them.

When Shane opened the door, a delivery boy stood there with a floral arrangement. "Delivery, sir, for Hope Walker."

A card stood on a holder higher than the flowers. Shane gave the boy a tip and took the arrangement. He didn't hesitate to read the card:

Happy birthday, kiddo. Enjoy.

Love, Mark

Mark. The friend from Wasco. The friend Hope had dated. Why the hell had he signed the card "Love"?

Close friends do that, the logical voice in Shane's mind told him.

The not-so-logical voice worried, *How close? Doesn't he know she's married? Did Hope tell him?*

Maybe she didn't. Maybe the guy still carried a torch. He obviously remembered details of her life, like her birthday.

Hope hadn't mentioned her birthday. Not once. Well, if Eloise hadn't reminded Shane, these flowers sure would have, and he'd have felt like a fool. Even now... He read the card again and looked at the arrangement.

Carnations and evergreens. How ordinary. Hope deserved roses and gardenias and orchids and... Shane set the
flowers in his office and called out, "Christopher. Come
here. We have to go out again."

The little boy came running. "Why?"

Shane stooped down and smiled at his son. "Because
we're going to find your mom a whole bunch of flowers.
And balloons that fly. What do you think?"

Christopher grinned and took Shane's hand. "Now."

"Yes, now. We might have to go to more than one flower
shop." He scooped his son up in his arms. "We're going to
give your mom a birthday she won't forget."

Hope stood on the porch with Jana before she opened the
door. "I really enjoyed this. I haven't been shopping with a
friend for a long time." She lifted the large shopping bag
filled with packages. "I'm just afraid I splurged."

"You bought a dress for Christmas and a few accesso-
ries. That is *not* splurging. Besides, that white dress was de-
signed with you in mind. Your coloring is perfect for white.
I'd fade in the dress."

The white silk with the delicate gold braid around the
collar and cuffs *was* special. Other than her wedding dress,
it was the prettiest garment she'd ever purchased. Maybe
she'd given in to the impulse because today was her birthday and only her Aunt El knew about it. She hadn't told
Shane because she didn't want him to feel obligated to buy
a gift.

"Jana, would you like to have supper with us? Or is
Adam expecting you?"

"Adam's always expecting me." Jana's eyes twinkled.
"But I'll see him soon enough. Come on. You can model the
dress for Shane."

"Oh, no. I think I'd rather surprise him on Christmas."
Hope opened the door and stepped inside.

Several voices called, "Surprise!"

Christopher came running to her. "Surprise, Mommy. Happy Birfday!"

Hope dropped her bag and hugged her son. The scent of flowers was strong in the living room. As she looked around at Adam, Aunt El and Jana's mom, she realized every available surface held a bouquet or basket of flowers. When she saw the vase of yellow roses, tears welled up in her eyes. Besides the roses, there were daylilies, poinsettias, mums, even some exotic-looking flowers she'd never seen. Helium balloons floated in bunches in the corners of the room. She leaned over to hug Christopher again and tried to compose herself.

Feeling a hand on her shoulder, she straightened. Shane's brown gaze held hers. "Happy Birthday, Hope."

The tears rolled down her cheeks and she couldn't manage a word.

Gently, Shane brushed the tears away from her cheeks. "C'mon now. You've got to say something or Christopher will think we didn't do a good enough job."

"Did you do this?"

"I had some help. Wait until you see the cake Eloise baked."

"The flowers are lovely, especially the yellow roses."

He took her hand. "I'm glad you like them."

Hope gazed down at their entwined fingers and loved the feeling of her hand in his. He tugged. "You have presents to open. Come see what everyone has brought you."

Hope had dreaded today. Without her mother, she would have skipped another birthday. Then Jana had asked her to go shopping. Now this... The tears resurfaced.

Shane lowered himself beside her on the sofa as everyone found a seat, commenting on Hope's surprise. The couch was plenty long, but his hip lodged next to hers, his jeans brushed the fabric of her slacks. Her breath came faster as Shane picked up a package from the coffee table and laid it on her lap. "This is from Christopher."

Hope removed the blue stick-on bow from the shoebox. Shane had probably found the box for Christopher, and from the way the bow was positioned, her son had attached it. She lifted the lid.

One of her son's prize stones sat in one corner. It was shiny and black, about as large as a golf ball. Taking it out of the box, she set it in her palm. "Thank you, honey. I'll put it on Nana's vanity so I can look at it often."

Christopher pointed to the folded piece of paper in the bottom of the box. "Open that."

Hope lifted the paper and opened it. The picture was a finger painting, mostly blue and green with a blob of yellow. "How pretty!"

Christopher explained, "It's the sky, an' grass, an' the sun."

Hope gave her son a huge hug. "I like it very much. We can hang it on the refrigerator."

As Jana took Matthew from Adam, she said, "Open the pink one next."

Hope tore the paper from the large gift box. Inside, she found a tooled-leather pocketbook. "Oh, my, Jana. It's beautiful!"

"Actually, I narrowed the choice down to two, and Adam made the final decision."

Hope turned toward Shane's friend. "You have excellent taste, Adam."

He grinned and his cheeks flushed. "Jana taught me everything I know. At least about shopping," he added with a wink for his wife.

Jana's mom handed Hope a basket filled with different types of teas. "Jana told me you enjoy unusual flavors."

Hope was touched by the woman's thoughtfulness. "I'll try one at breakfast. Thank you."

Next, Hope unwrapped a box from her aunt. It was a powder blue jogging suit, the type of outfit she liked to wear to lounge in for the evening. Hope went to her aunt, hugged her and kissed her. "You're so good to me," she murmured.

Eloise whispered in her ear, "I promised your mom I'd watch over you. You're the daughter I never had."

Settled once again on the sofa, Hope brushed the wetness from her cheek.

Shane leaned forward and carefully lifted a large flat box, placing it on Hope's lap. "This is from me."

As she pulled the bow from the box, her fingers trembled. Shane helped her push the paper from the box. Lifting the lid, she stared at a framed picture containing ten different poses of Christopher. It was a montage of photos of different shapes and sizes of their son swinging in the backyard, getting a drink from a water fountain, running in a nearby park, licking an ice-cream cone. One picture after another of a happy little boy.

Hope could think of only one thing to show her appreciation. She threw her arms around Shane's neck and gave him a sweetly tender kiss. She didn't expect his arms to go around her, but they did. She didn't expect his hold to tighten, but it did. She didn't expect his lips to part, or the kiss to deepen. And she didn't expect the heat curling in her womb as he kissed her long and hard in front of the guests gathered to celebrate her birthday. When he finally broke away, he looked a little dazed himself.

She suddenly felt awkward with everyone looking on and smiling broadly. "Thank you," she murmured. "I love it."

"Daddy took *lots* of pictures," Christopher supplied.

Shane cleared his throat. "I have a pack of snapshots I didn't use in the frame. I'll give them to you later," he said.

With her heart still thudding in her ears, she wasn't sure what to say or do next. Eloise stepped into the silence. "Time to eat. Everything is ready in the kitchen. And don't be shy. Shane bought enough for three birthday parties."

Adam stood first. "I'll try to make a dent."

The others laughed and followed him to the kitchen, Christopher holding little Matthew's hand and guiding the toddler in the right direction.

Shane stood and offered Hope his hand. She took it and smiled. Shane smiled back. Her heart took an excited leap and she felt truly happy.

Two hours later, Adam and his family left. Eloise cleared one of the trays, packing leftovers into a plastic container. Hope snitched a pickle from one of the dishes. "Shane thought of everything, didn't he?" she asked her aunt, still amazed he'd gone to so much trouble.

"I offered to help him plan, but once I reminded him of your birthday, all he wanted me to do was bake the cake."

He hadn't remembered on his own. That wasn't so surprising. Yet once her aunt had reminded him, had he felt obligated to throw her a party? Shane took his obligations seriously.

Christopher ran into the kitchen and stopped at the table, chocolate-cake crumbs decorating his upper lip. Shane came in after him. "I told Christopher he could have one more pretzel, then it's time for bed."

Shane's gaze found Hope's. He crooked his finger at her and his expression was serious. "I want to show you something."

Hope followed him to his office where he switched on the light and motioned to the flower arrangement on the desk.

"Shane, you already bought me a roomful of flowers."

"These aren't from me."

His deep voice sent shivers down her spine. She flipped open the card and read it. Shane was watching her closely.

"Does he buy you flowers often?"

There was no point evading Shane; she had nothing to hide. "Usually on my birthday. Sometimes on Valentine's Day."

"You're married now."

"I know. Mark knows. I wrote to him, telling him about our marriage, thanking him for sending the boxes I couldn't fit into the car. Shane, I told you before that Mark and I are friends. Just as you and Jana are friends." She laid the card on the desk.

His smile was wry. "Somehow, it doesn't seem the same." Stepping closer to her, he asked, "Will you write to him again?"

Her pulse raced, the room got hot and every nerve in her body came alive with Shane's closeness. "That would be the polite thing to do." Trying for a light tone, she teased, "I could write you a note, too."

He tipped up her chin. "I'd rather have the kind of thank-you I got after you opened your presents."

The pad of his thumb traced her upper lip so gently, so sensuously, she trembled. He murmured, "Happy Birthday, Hope," a moment before his lips sought hers.

It was a possession, a branding, a desire to change this marriage of convenience into something more. She surrendered to the possession, gave in to it, encouraged it, encouraged Shane to take more, want more, trust more. She responded to each stroke of his tongue as her body melted into his.

"Hope, do you want me to freeze some of the cake? I can— Oh. Sorry."

Shane broke away, and Hope opened her eyes in time to see her aunt scurrying out of the room. But this time, when she gazed into Shane's eyes, he didn't move away. In fact, his hand still rested on the small of her back.

"We have to put Christopher to bed." His voice was husky with the desire they'd shared.

"Shane, thank you for the flowers, the present, the party."

"You're welcome."

The gentle touch of his hand on her back, the golden lights in his eyes and the small smile on his lips told her more than words that he hadn't planned her birthday out of obligation. He cared. And maybe soon, that caring would become love.

Chapter Eight

"Fifteen. Sixteen. Seventeen." Hope counted slowly, giving Christopher time to find what he considered a good hiding place. He loved to play hide-and-seek, especially upstairs where he could slide under a bed or behind a drape.

Drapes and a bed brought Shane's room to mind. Maybe soon she'd be sharing it with him, maybe soon they'd truly be husband and wife. Her birthday party last night had been proof that he cared—and maybe more than cared.

After the kiss Eloise had interrupted, Hope thought Shane might invite her to his room. Though he'd kissed her again before he turned in, she could still see lingering doubts in his eyes, and she realized he was more vulnerable than he'd ever let her see. But they'd taken a few giant steps toward each other. She could wait until he trusted her again.

No longer hearing Christopher shuffling into a place to hide, she finished her counting. "Eighteen, nineteen, twenty. Here I come, ready or not."

Hope peeked outside the bathroom where she'd waited. She suspected Christopher might be in his favorite hiding place, but in the name of the game she looked carefully around his room. "No Christopher," she said in a loud voice. Stopping at the door to her bedroom, she called, "Christopher, where are you?" and heard a giggle. Her guess was correct. Going to the walk-in closet, she opened the door. Slowly, she separated clothes on the rod to peer behind them. "Christopher's not here, either. Maybe he's in his dad's room."

She heard the giggle again.

One side of the closet held blouses, skirts and sweaters. Underneath them stood a round wicker clothes hamper. Her son had wedged himself behind it, but his feet protruded.

"Why, I think I see a sneaker that doesn't belong in here." She wiggled his foot, and he giggled again. "I think I see a stocking, and a leg, and..." She pushed the hamper out of the way. "There's Christopher!"

When she tickled his tummy, he laughed and said, "You found me, Mommy."

She lifted him out of the corner. "You bet I did. I'll always find you. And just in time, too. Teddy told me he's ready for his nap."

"Did not."

She tickled Christopher again and set him outside the closet. "Did, too. Go to the bathroom, then I'll read you a story."

Hope was aware that her son was slowly growing out of nap times. Sometimes, she'd peek in and find him paging through a stack of books. Other times, he'd be running his cars over his pillow or talking to Teddy. But many days she still found him fast asleep.

She read him a story, kissed him and had partially closed his door when the doorbell rang. Shane answered it, and she heard voices, both male and female. Jana had left for the day. Maybe she'd forgotten something.

Suddenly, Shane's voice came up the stairs. "Hope. Can you come down for a few minutes?"

When she descended the steps, Shane, Harv and a pretty woman who looked to be about Harv's age were standing in the living room. Harv was grinning from ear to ear. "I wanted you to join us because I want to ask you and Shane a favor."

Hope crossed to Shane and stood beside him.

"But first, I want to introduce you to Bernadette."

Hope extended her hand. "It's nice to meet you."

Bernadette, a tall redhead with beautiful green eyes, gently gripped Hope's hand. "Harv told me how you assured him Shane would find me and how your words kept him going." She gave Harv a loving smile.

Hope glanced at Shane. He frowned and she realized they both remembered how he'd scolded her the last time Harv was here. "Harv thought I was Shane's partner that day."

"I'm sorry I mistook you for Shane's partner. I've never met her. But it's much nicer that you're Shane's wife. It'll make my idea more attractive, I hope."

Shane motioned to the sofa and they all sat. "What idea is that?" he asked.

"Bernie and I are getting married. We've wasted enough time. We want to do it as soon as possible and in style. How would you two like to fly to Las Vegas with us tomorrow? I know it's short notice, and Christmas is less than a week away, but it would only be overnight. You can be our witnesses at the ceremony. We'll have a nice dinner and stay overnight and fly back the next morning. What do you say?"

Hope thought Shane would turn down Harv's offer right away, but instead he seemed to be thinking about it. He turned to Hope. "You're finished with the shopping and baking, right?"

"I have some wrapping left. That's about it. Why? Do you want to go?"

"You didn't get a honeymoon."

Her mind went into overdrive. "You mean...?"

"I mean, it would be nice to get away overnight and relax before the holidays. If you think Christopher won't mind staying with Eloise."

"Oh, I don't think he'll mind. Not for just one night. We can ask him when he gets up."

"Harv, we're honored you asked us. Can I call you in a couple of hours and give you our answer?" Shane asked.

"Well, sure. That'll be fine."

After they saw Harv and Bernadette to the door, Shane closed it and turned toward Hope. "Would you like to go? Harv kind of put us both on the spot."

"It would be nice to spend some time alone with you—without Christopher, I mean. We could concentrate on us."

Shane took her hand, held it in his palm and smoothed his fingers over hers. "I'd like to concentrate on us."

Her heart soared. This was the moment she'd been waiting for—Shane willing to believe in her again, in them. *Las Vegas, here we come.*

The bellboy smiled when he looked at the tip Shane handed him. "Thank you, sir. Anything else you need . . ."

"We're fine. Thank you." He closed the door on the young man.

Hope picked up her garment bag to hang it in the closet. Shane took it from her. "I'll do that."

His leg brushed hers, khaki slacks against her navy jumpsuit. They'd been touching more lately. Not jumping apart and letting the sensations linger—at home, in Harv's private plane, as they checked into the hotel. It was tantalizing and frustrating at the same time.

Shane crossed to the closet and hung up the garment bag. "We have two hours before the ceremony. What would you like to do?"

Hope's gaze met his across the two double beds.

His brown eyes sparked with gold, and she knew they were both thinking the same thing. But the first move had to be his. She wouldn't ask him to make love to her; she wouldn't beg for his trust.

"We could look around," she suggested. "Take a walk. I've never been to Las Vegas."

"At night it's lit up like a Christmas tree. All year-round. But we can walk around now if you'd like."

They left the hotel, and Hope took in everything—the desert, the marquees, the people on the street. She smiled at passersby, and they smiled back. Shane guided her past resorts, restaurants, and wedding chapels. When they returned to their room, Hope dropped onto one of the beds. "Whew! This is some place, isn't it?"

He smiled. "Nice place to visit but you wouldn't want to live here?"

She smiled back. "Something like that." She paused, and chose her words carefully. "I'd like to take a shower. Uh..."

"You go ahead. I'll get mine when you're finished." He picked up the ice bucket on the dresser. "I'll go for ice. Would you like anything to drink?"

"Juice of some kind if they have it."

He nodded and went out the door.

Hope let out a pent-up breath. They were being so careful with each other. As if they were on their first date. Maybe they were.

She had packed light—the Christmas dress for the ceremony and dinner, jeans and a blouse for their return trip, and a satin nightgown and robe. Wishful thinking perhaps, but just in case...

Taking shampoo, brush and comb from the pocket of the garment bag, she took her robe from its hanger and went into the bathroom. In the shower, she let the hot water beat on the back of her neck. She hadn't realized how much tension she was holding there. When she finished showering, she used the hair dryer on the wall to dry her hair.

She opened the door and stepped into the bedroom.

Shane was sitting in the chair by the window, riffling through a newspaper, sipping a cola. His terry robe lay on one bed. "I got you orange juice. They..."

Gazing at her above the newspaper, his eyes became dark and dangerous.

She cleared her throat. "I...uh...can put on my makeup at the vanity out here if you want to shower."

He folded the newspaper in half and laid it on the table. When he stood, she backed up. He picked up his robe and came toward her, anyway. Stopping in front of her, his gaze started at her feet and slowly moved up her body until it lingered on her lips, finally her eyes.

"If I kiss you now, we'll never make it to Harv and Bernie's wedding."

Her hands trembled and her knees wobbled. "They'd be disappointed."

"Unfortunately, that's true." He slipped by her, but stopped at the threshold of the bathroom. "It would be a good idea if you're dressed when I come out."

Hope sank to the bed. She had the feeling this was going to be an evening she'd never forget.

She'd applied makeup, dressed and was clipping a gold barrette in her hair when the bathroom door opened. Making herself stay facing forward, she took a peek at Shane in the vanity mirror. His still-damp hair was darker and brushed to one side with tendrils dangling at the nape of his neck. The V of the robe's lapels displayed a matt of light brown chest hair. The hem of the garment stopped at his thighs, powerful thighs that even in shorts didn't look as sexy as they did below the robe.

When he crossed to the closet, Hope slipped into the bathroom again and closed the door. There, she waited until he had time to dress. She felt foolish, but also awkward, hopeful and excited. Finally, she opened the door.

Shane was tying his tie when she crossed to the dresser. She opened her purse and dropped her lipstick inside. Suddenly, she felt Shane close, his hand on her shoulder. Gently, he turned her toward him. "You look beautiful." He traced the gold braiding on her collar. "Like a Christmas angel."

"And you look very handsome in your suit. It reminds me of our wedding day." Shane's hair tumbled over his forehead. Hope couldn't keep herself from touching him, from pushing it back.

He took her hand and brought it to his lips. They were warm and sensual on her palm. "We have a wedding to attend." His murmur was a husky reminder that they were in Las Vegas for a reason. They would have to deal with their feelings and desires later.

Hope marveled at the circus atmosphere in Las Vegas. Weddings were a breed unto themselves—from the drive-up window where couples exchanged vows in their car to the chapels where Elvis impersonators performed solos. A limousine had met them at the airport when they arrived, and picked them up again that evening. Shane had told her on the plane that it was Harv's usual mode of transportation when traveling.

Now, sitting beside his fiancée, Harv pointed to the bottle of champagne chilling in its magnum. "We'll break that open after the ceremony." He took Bernadette's hand and put it on his knee. "It was only a month or so ago that these folks got hitched. Got any advice, Shane?"

Shane shook his head. "I'm no expert."

Bernie addressed Hope. "I guess what I'm worried about most is both of us being so set in our ways, we'll drive each other crazy."

"As long as you love each other, you can get past that. You can compromise," Hope answered, believing it.

Harv squeezed Bernie's hand. "Havin' doubts, darlin'?"

Her eyes found his. "Not about loving you."

His expression got serious. "Then I agree with Hope. The rest will settle itself. We've waited too long not to be together now."

As usual, Hope couldn't tell anything from Shane's expression. Was he thinking about the last four years or the next four?

The chapel they entered was less gaudy than the few she and Shane had seen that afternoon, and it was no bigger than Shane's living room. The inside was painted white, and white doves and silver bells hung from the ceiling. Five wooden benches flanked the left and the right. An aisle with a red runner divided the room and led to the dais where a podium stood.

The minister met them at the door. Harv shook his hand and introduced him to his bride-to-be and their witnesses. The limousine driver presented Bernie with a bouquet of daisies and orchids. With her cream taffeta, street-length dress, her upswept red hair and her sparkling green eyes, she was a stunning bride.

The driver handed Hope a smaller bouquet of daisies and roses. Her hand trembled as she took it. In a way, she felt as if she were getting married all over again.

Hope stood beside Bernie while Shane took his place beside Harv. The minister's words, as well as the vows Bernie and Harv exchanged, were similar to those in Hope and Shane's ceremony. As the couple slipped rings onto each other's fingers, Shane's gaze met Hope's. She thought she saw sadness in the depths of his brown eyes, but she wasn't sure. She wanted to see joy and hope and the love she felt for him. But he was still guarding himself.

When Harv and Bernie kissed each other, the love and passion between them was obvious. It was a few moments until they broke apart, smiling sheepishly. After Harv thanked the minister, he gathered his new bride close to his side, grinned and said, "Let's celebrate! Wait until you see the dinner I've set up."

Back at the hotel, the maître d' showed them to a table in the dining room far enough from the orchestra to be private, but close enough to enjoy the music. Harv pulled out a chair for Bernie while Shane did the same for Hope. Another bottle of champagne sat beside Harv's chair.

"I hope you like lobster tail and filet mignon. Cherries jubilee for dessert, so save some room."

Harv flew his plane all over the United States in conjunction with his computer networks consulting business. His stories about clients and the glitches he ran into kept conversation flowing during dinner.

Except . . . as Hope dipped chunks of lobster into butter and transferred the fork to her mouth, she caught Shane watching her intently. She couldn't keep her eyes from his strong hands and agile fingers as he used the steak knife and brought the meat to his lips. She felt so close to him, yet so far away. It was a strange sensation.

As he put down his fork and pushed his plate away, his knee brushed hers under the table. Hope didn't move. His gaze collided with hers, and she held her breath. The intensity practically stopped her heart. He pushed his chair back and stood.

"Harv, if you and Bernie would excuse us, I'd like to dance with my wife."

Harv chuckled. "I understand. You'll know when dessert's arrived by the flames over here. But if you're too engrossed in what you're doing, we'll understand."

Shane extended his hand to Hope. She took it. He kept his palm on the small of her back as he guided her to the dance floor. Only a few couples were dancing to the slow music. Hope had never danced with Shane before. They'd always spent their time talking or hiking in the canyons. Dressing up and going out hadn't been important to either of them.

But tonight, dancing seemed to be the perfect thing to do.

Shane took Hope's right hand as he slipped his arm around her waist and drew her toward him. He held her close. Very close.

"What flames are Harv talking about?" she asked.

"You've never eaten cherries jubilee?"

She shook her head and her chin brushed his lapel.

"Basically, the cherries are cooked with brandy then lit until the flames dissolve. That gets rid of the alcohol and leaves the flavor. Then the cherries are served over vanilla ice cream. A simple dessert with a fancy name and a fancy presentation. They light the cherries right at the table. It's some show."

She laughed. "I guess we *will* know when they serve dessert."

Hope's steps followed Shane's as if they'd danced together often. His breath whispered against her forehead as he said, "You were distracting me at dinner."

"I was?"

"Uh-huh." Leaning back, he didn't loosen his hold. "The way you eat lobster is sinful."

She felt a blush crawl up her neck. "I like lobster."

"I could tell. You ate it slowly, savoring each morsel. And when the butter coated your lower lip..." He brought their bodies into even closer contact. "I could only think about kissing you, and letting you enjoy me like you were enjoying that lobster."

She went hot, then cold, then hot again. His words were exciting her, making her want him even more than she already did. She had the feeling he knew it. "I watched you cutting your steak."

"And?"

"And I remembered how capable your hands are, how gentle, how... arousing."

"Why, Hope Walker, I think you're trying to turn me on."

"And what are you trying to do?"

He made a slow circle on the small of her back, pressed his thighs against hers and teasingly caught her earlobe with his lips. If he hadn't been holding her, her legs would have buckled. After suckling her earlobe, he placed a gentle kiss on her neck. "I guess I'm trying to tell you I don't want us to sleep in separate beds tonight. How do you feel about it?"

Feel? She felt as if she were suspended somewhere between heaven and the sublime. He wanted her. He wanted her in his bed and in his life. "I'd like to share your bed with you, and anything else you want to share."

She felt him stiffen. "Hope, just because we sleep together doesn't mean all our problems are solved."

"What are our problems, Shane?"

He trailed his finger down her cheek. "Damned if I know right now. All I can think about is undressing you, kissing you, touching you. How fast do you think we can eat dessert?"

His chagrin and frustration made her smile. "I'm pretty good at downing ice cream. Three minutes, tops."

"If you eat ice cream too fast, it can give you a headache."

"Then I'll be sure and take at least five minutes. Because, Shane, I'm not going to have a headache tonight."

The flare of desire in his eyes was more potent than any flames on a dessert. He kissed her with a slow lingering tenderness, creating an ache inside her that could only be satisfied one way, soon, in Shane's bed.

When he lifted his head, fire leaped between them. Hope knew she was going to get burned, but she didn't care because she'd decided to give anything to Shane that he wanted. In giving, she would find his love.

He glanced over her head. "The waiter is standing at the table. We'd better go back."

Hope didn't remember much about dessert. The ice cream was cold on her tongue, the cherries warm and sweet, but not as sweet as Shane's kiss. He kept watching her, particularly her lips as she spooned in the dessert. She tried to keep her mind on the conversation, but the best she could do was add a short comment here or there.

Finally, they were finished. Harv set a time for them to meet the next morning, and then she and Shane were riding up to their room in the elevator. He stood a few inches away from her. She wanted to touch him, to feel the heat, to make sure it was still there, but she didn't feel that freedom with him yet. Maybe after tonight...

Shane slid the card into the lock, opened the door and turned on the light. Hope didn't know what to do next. Shane had made himself clear when they were dancing, but now...

He slipped off his suit jacket and tossed it over the chair. Then he opened the top button of his shirt and tugged down his tie. It hung loose around his neck. He mowed his hand through his hair and then looked at her. She saw the desire, but something was missing, something they'd lost.

He crossed to her and stood before her, the nerve in his jaw working, his cologne wrapping around her, the swell of tension between them rising to a screaming pitch against the background of silence. "I want you, Hope. So badly that I couldn't touch you in the elevator because I knew we wouldn't have made it back to the room. I don't want to scare you. I don't want your needs to get trampled because—"

Shane had been a patient, gentle lover...the first time. She laid her finger over his lips. "I'm not afraid of you, Shane."

He sucked in a breath and crushed her to him. His lips were anything but patient. His tongue speared into her mouth taking her breath away. While he kissed her, his hands found the zipper at the back of her dress and it scraped down the track. There was a harshness about the quickness of it. But there was nothing harsh in Shane's kiss, just unleashed passion that he'd denied for too long. She reached for the buttons of his shirt, as eager to touch him as he was to touch her.

With a groan, he pulled away. She let her dress fall from her shoulders to the carpet. The expression on his face was pained. She'd worn nothing but her bra and lacy panties under the satin-lined dress. He stared at her, his cheeks flushed by the heat bursting between them. ''I remember everything about you. I remember...'' He passed his hand over the slight roundness of her belly, the swell of her hips. ''Having Christopher has made you more beautiful.''

His fingertips on her skin sent thrills through her. She reached for his belt buckle, but he stilled her hands, covering them with one of his. ''You really haven't been with anyone else?''

His question hurt her because he was doubting whether or not she'd told him the truth. All she could do was reassure him again. ''You were the first, Shane, and the only one.''

Closing his eyes, he brought her hands to his lips and kissed her fingertips. Then he wrapped her arms around his waist, and kissed her again. Hard...with a possessive intensity that was raw need. She passed her hands up and down his back, appreciating the strength, loving the feel of him. She felt a shudder rip through him. Apparently, her touch was as potent as his.

Unhooking her bra, he backed her up toward the bed. Then he swept her into his arms and laid her down. She watched him swiftly undo his belt buckle and drop his pants. With a shrug, his shirt landed on the floor. When he skimmed off his briefs, she just stared. Shane was powerful and male and looking at her as if he wanted to devour her. She held out her arms to him.

He came to her and skimmed her panties down her legs. When he brought his mouth to her breasts, she cried out in pleasure. His hands teased and taunted, increasing the ache inside her until loving Shane became foremost in her mind. He tested her for her readiness with his fingers. And then...

His heat was gone, so were his lips, his hands. "Shane?" She heard the nightstand drawer open.

He ripped open the foil packet and prepared himself.

"Shane, I'm on the Pill. As soon as we decided to get married, I—"

"Better safe than sorry." His voice was husky with need but clear in his message. Christopher would be their only child. He hadn't changed his mind about bringing children into the world. She had expected that, that's why she'd gone on the Pill. But it was the rest of the message that stabbed her heart. He still didn't trust her.

Before she had time to think about it, before she could feel the full extent of the pain, he rose above her and kissed her again. This was the man she loved, the man she wanted to love for the rest of their lives. She opened her arms and her heart to him. When he surged into her, the pleasure was so intense, she gripped his buttocks to urge him deeper. He thrust and thrust again until she cried out, flying over the edge of desire into joy, yet there was anguish, too—because Shane was still protecting himself from loving her.

As soon as he heard her cry of release, Shane let himself go. But even then, as he found completion, they weren't complete. They were still two separate people, lovers now, but not fully loving. How could she prove to Shane that he could trust her? How could she earn his love?

Chapter Nine

Shane sorted through the mail, giving the business letters to Jana. "Here's something for Hope. I'll be right back."

He went to the kitchen and sniffed appreciatively. Chocolate chip cookies. Hope was baking them so Christopher could leave a few for Santa Claus. She was trying to make Christmas Eve a special night.

Hope transferred cookies from the racks on the table to a can. Coming up behind her, Shane breathed in the scent of her shampoo mixed with a more womanly scent that turned him on instantly. It didn't take much these days. With Hope, it never had. Three nights ago in Las Vegas, they'd come together in passion. He'd felt changed in some way ever since.

Brushing her hair behind her ear, he dropped a string of kisses along her collarbone. "Hey, pretty lady. I hope you're going to leave one out for my snack."

He felt her tremble as he pressed against her. She was so responsive to him. Sleeping with her, reaching for her in the middle of the night, had become a habit in a few short days.

Hope turned in his arms. "A few? If I give you one, you'll want six. I know you and chocolate chip cookies."

"What about a kiss, instead?"

"One or six?" she teased, taking a tremulous breath.

"I'll start with one." He tried to keep the kiss teasing and gentle and light, but as soon as he tasted her, he wanted much more than a sample kiss. Christopher was napping upstairs, but Jana was close by in the office.

Calling on all the restraint he possessed, he ended the kiss and lifted his head.

Hope smiled. "I guess I could give you a plate of cookies to share with Jana."

"Ah, the bribery worked. Little do you know, but my partner's leaving soon so I'll have them all to myself."

Hope poked him in the ribs. "I'll say goodbye before I go upstairs to wrap presents."

Shane raised the envelope he'd been holding in his hand. "I have something for you besides a kiss."

Hope glanced at the letterhead and took the envelope from him, sliding her finger under the flap and opening it. Withdrawing the sheet of paper, she unfolded it. "My final course schedule. Everything is set." With a quick grin, she said, "I'm really going back to school."

"You're excited about it."

"Yes. And grateful. I appreciate this opportunity, Shane. When I'm finished, I'll be able to teach and maybe make a difference."

He had no doubt she'd make a good teacher. Marrying him had made it possible for her to follow her dream. Automatically, the usual doubts about her motives niggled at him. He tried to nudge them away.

"I'd better get back to Jana. The sooner we go through that last batch of letters, the sooner she'll get home." Shane left the kitchen, forgetting about the cookies.

In the office, he sank into his swivel chair.

"What happened?" Jana asked.

"Nothing happened."

"You've been different lately. I thought maybe it was the season, but my guess is your good mood has more to do with you and Hope. Except now, you left happy and came back sad."

"I'm trying to get my life in order and make a marriage with Hope. We're having our ups and downs. That's all."

"What's going on, Shane? I spend a lot of time in this office with you, and I think I know you. You're fighting some kind of battle and you won't let anyone help."

"Nobody can help."

"Not even Hope?"

"Hope's a part of the battle. We're getting closer. Sometimes it feels right, sometimes it's damned uncomfortable."

"What's uncomfortable?"

"What I feel when I'm with her. The things she stirs up."

"What things?"

He could blow his top at Jana for prying or he could think about her question. The answers came in rapid succession. "Feelings. Memories. My father leaving. My mother taking her life."

"Your first son."

"Yes, Davie. Christopher reminds me of him, yet he has Hope's smile and hair color, her enthusiasm for anything new."

"But you sound as if that hurts you instead of bringing you pleasure."

"It does. I don't know why. It just does. That's what's as confusing as hell."

"And as lonely," Jana offered softly.

"I'm used to being alone."

"Being alone and being lonely are two different things."

The phone rang, and Jana picked it up. From the quality of her smile, Shane knew who was on the other end before she covered the mouthpiece and said, "It's Adam."

To her husband, she explained, "We have a stack of letters to go through yet. And I'd like to get some of the names into the computer."

Shane picked up the phone on his desk. "She'll be home as soon as she can. It's Christmas Eve and she should be with you and Matthew. Hang up your stocking, Hobbs. Maybe Santa will come up with that Jaguar you've had your eye on." Shane hung up the phone.

Jana laughed. "Adam? I guess Shane's saying he'll finish up here. I'll leave now. And when I get home, we'll talk about this item you must have asked Santa about but forgot to mention to me." She laughed again at something her husband said, tenderly murmured, "I love you," and hung up. Then she grinned at Shane. "He said he'll get you later."

Hope appeared in the doorway to the office with a plate of cookies and put them on her husband's desk. "Jana, I wanted to wish you a merry Christmas before I go upstairs."

"Merry Christmas to you, too. Do you have plans for tomorrow evening?" Jana asked.

Shane chuckled. "Just playing with Christopher's toys."

"Then why don't you come over? Mom's cooking up a storm. Adam's girls will be there, too."

Shane looked at Hope and saw from her expression that she'd like to go. "Around six?"

Jana took her purse from the bottom desk drawer. "Six is good." Coming out from behind the desk, she gave Shane a hug. "I hope Santa brings you everything you wish for." Releasing Shane, she went to Hope and gave her a hug. "And you, too."

Hope said to Shane, "I'll see Jana to the door."

As the two women walked through the living room, Hope offered, "I'll bring along some fudge I made, if that's okay."

"If you have any left."

"I made two batches. Christopher and Shane don't know about the second one."

Jana laughed. "Bring your aunt along if she'd like to come."

"I'm sure she will. She's coming for dinner and probably will stay through the afternoon." Hope opened the door for Jana. "I want to thank you for your friendship. It means more than you know."

"You're an easy person to be friends with. Have a wonderful Christmas Eve. I'll see you tomorrow."

Hope closed the door. Tonight would be wonderful if she had anything to say about it—a festive dinner, hanging their stockings, reading Christopher holiday stories. After their son went to bed, maybe she and Shane could exchange their presents... then fall asleep in each other's arms.

Shane was typing information into the computer when the fax machine beeped. One piece of paper hummed out, then a second and a third. He swiveled toward the machine and lifted them out.

The first sheet was a letter from Hope's lawyer. Shane would have just collected the papers and taken them upstairs to Hope except one phrase caught his eye and the number on the line shocked him. The printed words jumped at him. Her lawyer urged her to accept the offer for her mother's land in Arizona, an offer that spread over six digits!

As Shane read the letter, then looked over the contract, anger rose in him, hot and fierce. One thought after another ran through his mind, but the primary fact fueling his rage was clear—Hope had lied to him. Again.

The anger blurred the print in front of his eyes; it blinded him to gentler emotions that had been growing since his wedding day. The pain in his heart swelled until he rammed his fist on the desk. Damn her! Damn her for not telling him the truth.

With his hand closed on the papers, he mounted the steps slowly, dreading facing Hope, yet knowing he had no choice. Fleetingly, he thought about waiting to confront her, playing out Christmas Eve as if nothing had happened. But he wasn't an actor and he could never hide the betrayal he was feeling. Besides, Hope only had forty-eight hours to decide if she would accept the offer. Why wouldn't she? Unless she knew the property could possibly bring in even more!

In his soul, he knew why she'd kept the truth from him, but he wanted to hear her say it.

Hope sat on Shane's bed, Christmas wrapping paper and bows scattered around her. She folded the paper on one end of a box and secured it with tape. As she looked up, she smiled.

But her smile faded when she saw his expression. "What's wrong?"

"Nothing's wrong. At least not for you. You're sitting pretty. Your lawyer just faxed you an offer on that plot of land in Arizona. Some 'little' plot." Shane dropped the papers on the bed.

Picking them up, she skimmed the letter. "Oh-my-gosh! I never expected anything like this."

"Drop the act, Hope."

Her chin came up. "Excuse me?"

"You can cut the surprise. A little plot of land, you said. Some plot of land. Did you expect me to *not* find out about it? I guess I never mentioned I told your lawyer he could use my fax number to send paperwork to you. If I hadn't made the offer, maybe I wouldn't have found out."

"Just what are you accusing me of?" Her voice had risen to match his.

"I'm accusing you of deceit. Again. You're getting good at it, Hope. Sorry I interfered."

"You're not making sense, Shane. I didn't know the land was worth this. I thought Mom and Dad had bought it to build a small retirement place."

"It's ten acres, Hope. That's no 'little' plot of land."

"I didn't *know* it was ten acres. Don't you understand? I never knew exactly what it was."

"You expect me to believe that?"

"Why shouldn't you?"

"Because you lied to me before," he almost shouted, the pain of missing Christopher's first three years hurting so badly, he didn't think he would ever forget it.

"Oh, Shane. I thought you were beginning to forgive me. But you haven't even started. Why would I lie to you? Why would I keep this from you no matter how much it was worth?"

The sadness on her face seemed real. Yet . . . "You came to me with no job, practically nothing. You needed help."

Her back straightened and she held her head high. "I did not *need* help. I came to you so you could get to know your son . . . and because I still loved you."

How he wished he could believe that. His experience, his doubts about Hope's motives told him otherwise. "No. You knew if you had nothing, I'd take pity on you, I'd want to provide for you and our son."

"Pity? That's why you married me?" She seemed shocked.

He didn't care now if his words hurt her. He wanted her to feel the same pain he was feeling. "Sure, pity was part of it, along with wanting to be near my son."

He saw his words spear through her, he saw her quick intake of breath before she asked, "Do you think I wanted a father for our son so badly?"

"You love kids, Hope. You'd do anything for Christopher."

"No. You're wrong. I wouldn't marry a man who only married me out of pity. I have more self-respect than that."

"If I remember correctly, you were ready to throw your-self at me. I'm not sure how much self-respect you have."

Her face went white. "You seem to have this all figured out. So what was I going to do when you did find out how much the property was worth? As my husband, you would have found out eventually."

The answer was obvious to him and ready on his tongue. It had a bitter taste. "That property could have taken for-ever to sell. As your lawyer explains in his letter, this devel-opment company sees the potential in it. My guess is when the windfall came through, you were going to divorce me. You would no longer need me to finance your life, your ed-ucation, or Christopher's, for that matter."

"You are so wrong."

His hands balled into fists as he gave her the suspicions that had burdened him since her return, the suspicions that now seemed justified. "Not from where I'm standing. You didn't tell me you were pregnant. It took you until Chris-topher was more than three years old to tell me I had a son. Why? You lost your job and your mother... your only se-curity in this world...dies. You feel adrift. You know you'll get little money from her belongings, and you have nothing else except a valuable piece of land. The problem is, it's not valuable unless it sells, and you have no idea when that will be. So you come to me, to use me, until you and Christo-pher don't need me anymore. It's all so clear now."

Hope hopped up from the bed, her movement causing rolls of paper to tumble to the floor. "Clear? The only thing that's clear is how muddled your thinking is. The trouble is—I know better than to try and convince you otherwise because you're more stubborn than any mule!" Hurrying to the hallway, she headed for the stairs.

In a few quick strides, Shane snagged her arm. "Where are you going?"

"For a walk. To sort things out. To think about the real estate offer. To pray that when I come back, you'll be willing to listen to reason." On that note, she pulled away and hurried down the steps. The front door slammed, the sound reverberating through the house.

Shane sought refuge in his office and stared out the window, feeling numb. He didn't know what to believe anymore. He couldn't think. He couldn't feel. He could only ache without knowing why. The sun moved toward the west, its rays fading from the office. Without its warmth, the December air coming through the window became cooler.

He glanced at his watch. Christopher was usually up by now, peeking into the kitchen to see what his mother was cooking, or slipping into Shane's office to see what he was doing. Concerned, Shane went upstairs and pushed open the door to Christopher's room.

His son wasn't in his bed. Or in any other part of the room. Shane looked from corner to corner, from toy box to bookshelves. No Christopher. Maybe he was in Hope's room . . . what used to be Hope's room.

Shane pushed open the door and stepped inside. It still looked like her room. Her mother's perfume bottles sat on the vanity. A book she'd started before their trip to Las Vegas lay on the nightstand. A pair of black espadrilles sat by the chair. Her wicker handbag hung by its handle on the closet doorknob. Most of her belongings were still in this room. He hadn't suggested she move everything over to his and she hadn't asked. A pang of regret stung a place in his heart that hurt already.

He checked his room next, both bathrooms, and still didn't find his son. Worried, he called Christopher's name over and over then rushed downstairs. He examined every room, every corner. The kitchen door stood open. He pushed the screen door and plunged onto the back porch calling, "Christopher," over and over again.

* * *

Slowing her stride, Hope tried to calm herself, tried to believe she and Shane still had a chance. Why was he so determined to believe the worst of her? Why couldn't he take her at her word?

She didn't have an answer when she returned to the front door, out of breath, and still hurting. Taking a few deep breaths, she opened the door and went in.

Shane rushed in from the kitchen. "Have you seen Christopher?"

"Christopher? No. Why would— Where is he?" Her voice rose with the panic she saw on Shane's face.

"I don't know. I can't tell you to stay calm because I can't. God, Hope, what are we going to do? I've looked everywhere. I'm ready to call Jana and the police. What if he wandered into the yard and somebody took him?"

Shane was the private investigator, the former cop who knew all about the dark side, about what could go wrong rather than right. She'd taught Christopher boundaries. He couldn't have broken through all of them. "Tell me what happened."

Shane paced across the living room. "I went upstairs to get him up, and he wasn't there."

"He doesn't take a nap every day."

Shane stopped for a moment. "Of course he does. We put him in his room—"

Shaking her head, she explained, "Some days he falls asleep. Others, he reads or plays."

After a tense pause, Shane mowed his hand through his hair. "All right. Maybe he wasn't napping. But he should still be in his room."

"Not if he heard us arguing. Not if he got scared."

The worry in Shane's brown eyes changed to panic again. "So we're back to where he would go. Honest to God, Hope—"

"Did you check all his hide-and-seek hiding places?"

"*What* are you talking about?"

"When we play hide-and-seek. When you two play in the yard, he always hides behind the crepe myrtle or next to the shed or under the sliding board. He has hiding places in the house, too. We play while you're working."

"Where?" Shane was already heading for the stairs.

"Shane, if he's scared, I don't want to scare him more."

Shane stopped on the first step. "All right. I'm calm. Now show me."

Hope crossed to him and gave him a gentle push. "Look under your bed." His body tensed under her hands and she remembered every word of their disagreement. Then he climbed the steps, moving away from her touch and she sighed, telling herself to handle one crisis at a time.

Christopher wasn't under the bed or in the bathtub or behind his toy box. Hope went to the closet in her bedroom, Shane tight on her heels. Opening the door, she flicked on the light and almost collapsed from relief when she saw two small stockinged feet on the left side of the closet. She alerted Shane by pointing.

When he saw Christopher's feet, the relief on Shane's face was obvious. So was the love as he sat down on the floor.

Hope pushed aside her clothes and curled next to her son. "Watcha doin'?"

"Nothin'."

"We couldn't find you. We were very worried."

Shane tapped Christopher's foot because the three-year-old was staring at his lap and wouldn't look up. "You shouldn't hide from us."

"You yelled at Mommy." His big brown eyes were shiny, and Hope could imagine what Christopher's accusing look was doing to Shane.

"And I yelled back," she added. "Christopher, your dad and I had an argument. Adults do that sometimes. We didn't mean to scare you."

"You did."

Hope slipped her arm around him, tucking him close to her side. "We're sorry. Especially today. Christmas Eve is special. We want you to be happy, not afraid."

"Are you and Daddy still mad?"

She couldn't speak for Shane, and she wouldn't lie to their son. "We have to talk some more before we know. But I'll tell you what. Your dad and I will forget about being mad at each other until after Christmas. Christmas isn't a time for being mad. It's a time to give lots of love and hugs and kisses."

"And presents," Christopher added.

"And presents," Shane agreed, holding out his arms to his son. "C'mon, partner. Let's go get your sneakers. You and I can play ball while your mom gets supper ready."

Christopher moved from Hope's side and went willingly into Shane's arms. "Okay."

Shane's brown eyes met Hope's over Christopher's head. Nothing was settled, and the tension from their argument still vibrated between them. But they would both do whatever they could to make their son feel loved and secure.

Before Hope cleaned up the mess on Shane's bed, she called her lawyer to find out exactly what was going on with her mother's property. Expecting to get his answering machine or service, she was relieved when he answered himself.

"Just in the nick of time, Hope. My secretary left and I'm on my way out."

"I won't hold you up. I just wondered what you think of the contract, why they offered so much. I thought this was just an undeveloped plot of land. I never knew it was ten acres. I never knew it was worth so much."

"Jennie and I didn't know it could be worth that, either. A few months ago, you might have gotten a quarter of that sum. But you lucked out. A highway is going to be cutting through that area. The developer who wants to buy your property is planning a shopping center. I'd advise you to take the offer, Hope. It won't get much better than that."

"I still can't believe it."

"Believe it. A highway can transform rural property into prime real estate. The fax was just to let you look over the paperwork. You'll have to come into my office day after tomorrow and sign the contract. If you have any questions, make a list. I'll answer them for you then. You have a merry Christmas."

Hope wished him the same and said goodbye, not caring about the offer or the money. All she cared about was the way Shane perceived it.

As she prepared dinner, she peeked out the window and saw her husband and son playing ball. Shane rolled a ball across the grass. Christopher ran after it, picked it up in his pudgy little hands and tried to toss it back to Shane. The ball tossing turned into a game of tag and then as Shane stood by and watched, Christopher climbed up then slid down the sliding board.

When Hope called for them to wash up, Shane scooped up his son and put him on his shoulders until they got to the porch. She took the roast chicken out of the oven and had everything ready when Shane and Christopher came into the kitchen. Busyness held her fears at bay, at least for the time being.

The tension between her and Shane was almost palpable, but they talked with Christopher and kept conversation between themselves to a minimum. After dinner, they hung three stockings on the mantel. Finally, Christopher nestled between them on the sofa. Hope read the Christmas story from the Bible.

"An angel talked to the shepherds," Christopher said when Hope closed the book.

She kissed him on the top of his head. "Angels help guide us. Tomorrow morning, you tell us if you heard the Christmas angel."

With a sleepy nod, he mumbled, "I will."

By the time they put milk and cookies on the mantel for Santa, Christopher was yawning. Shane carried him piggy-back up the stairs. As with any three-year-old on Christmas Eve, he prolonged his bedtime ritual. But by the time Hope and Shane kissed him good-night, he hugged his teddy bear as his eyes closed in slumber.

Hope went downstairs, going over in her mind what she could say to Shane, how she could make him believe her. She'd taken a bag of small presents from the foyer closet and was placing them in Christopher's stocking when Shane came downstairs. His expression was serious; Hope didn't know what was going to happen next.

"Would you like something to drink?" he asked. "I'm going to get a brandy."

"No, thanks."

Shane unlocked the top of a bookcase. Inside stood a shelf of glasses and a few bottles of liquor. Hope hadn't even known it was there. She'd never looked inside. Shane opened one of the bottles, poured a small amount into a snifter and closed the cabinet. "It's my fault he got scared," he said. "What if he had found his way downstairs and out the door?"

She should have realized Shane would take responsibility for upsetting Christopher. "He knows the rules, Shane. He's never supposed to go outside alone."

Shane swirled the amber liquid in his glass. "When he's afraid, he might forget the rules. I just want to keep him safe, Hope. How can I do that?"

She couldn't keep away from Shane, she couldn't keep from standing close and wanting to erase the anguish from his eyes. "We'll keep him safe. We'll tell him everything he should know for his own good, and we'll protect him every way we can. But we can't lock him in a cocoon away from the real world."

Shane downed the brandy in two swallows, set the glass on the shelf, then held her by her shoulders. "Why can't we? Why can't we just keep him in here with us so we know he's safe?"

She searched his eyes, seeing the sadness and doubts, the fear and pain. "Because that's not letting him live."

"Dammit, Hope. Look how easy it would be to lose him. It could have happened today."

He was thinking of Christopher, but he was thinking of Davie, too. "Don't do this to yourself, Shane."

"You can say that now. But how forgiving would you be if Christopher had wandered outside? If something had happened?"

She closed her eyes and tried to imagine it. She couldn't. It was too painful. So she could only guess at the pain and guilt that Shane felt about Davie. Reaching out, she stroked his jaw. "You've got to let it go, Shane. Please, try to let it go."

She didn't know if he was trying to block out memories or create new ones when he kissed her. All she knew was that he was kissing her as if he needed her forever. There was a fever in the kiss and a desperation that made her heart trip. Something about it brought tears to her eyes.

The first kiss caught fire and gave birth to another... and another. The first touch led to another... and another. There were no more firsts between them as the sparks flew and their passion exploded. The brandy on Shane's tongue became intoxicating. He removed her sweat suit in the same amount of time it took for her to tug off his T-shirt and un-snap his jeans. Their clothes fell away as they tried to kiss more, touch more, feel more.

Shane's beard stubble rasped across her breast. Her nails scraped his back. As he took her down to the carpet, she wrapped her arms around his waist. When she lay back, he came with her. Bracing his arms on either side of her, he thrust into her with an anguished groan. Suddenly, she knew why tears had filled her eyes earlier and why they were filling them now. He wanted her, maybe he even needed her, but he was afraid to love her. She might never know his love. She might never know all of Shane.

In desperation, she gave herself to him. She kissed him and held him tight, trying to show him just how much she wanted, needed and loved him. Giving herself up to him, she let him give her pleasure. She climbed higher and higher with him, until they toppled together, holding on to each other as if they'd never let go.

But a few moments later, Shane did let go. He slid to his side and said like a judge pronouncing a sentence, "We didn't use protection."

Chapter Ten

Shane's accusations that she had kept the value of the property from him had hurt, but his doubts about the birth control cracked her heart. When he'd made love to her just now without additional protection, she'd thought maybe they had a chance. She'd thought maybe it was a conscious decision on his part to show her he could trust her. But apparently, passion had driven him, had driven them both, and it had had nothing to do with trust at all.

"I told you before, I'm on the Pill."

His silence was his response.

All the weeks of patience Hope had cultivated, all the loving thoughts she'd nurtured about time healing and time proving how much she loved Shane, lit a fuse leading directly to anger. Shane had been the angry one. She had deserved some of it. But she didn't deserve his constant lack of trust, and now she was angry, angrier than she'd ever been.

The surge of it almost left her breathless. "You're never going to believe I love you, are you?"

His voice was cold. "You told me you loved me four years ago then you called off the wedding."

They were back to that again. There was something else she wasn't seeing, something that went much deeper than leaving him at the altar. But right now, the anger sending adrenaline through her wouldn't give her the time to think it through.

"I loved you enough not to trap you, Shane."

He looked startled. She had never put it in those terms before. "You're so sure I would have seen it as a trap?"

"Yes. You see in black and white, good or bad. There's no gray, nor room for human imperfections. I made a mistake—a giant one, I'll grant you. I loved you so much, I didn't want to go into a marriage with you resenting me or a child you didn't want. I was thinking about all of us. But then I realized what a terrible mistake I'd made, and I told you about Christopher. You want to give me every kind of motive except the one that counts—I still loved you. But you can't believe that. You'd rather think I want a free ride, that I'm biding my time until I have enough money to leave again. Get real, Shane. What happens to my emotions and Christopher's in all that? Do you think I'd put him through all this willingly?"

Deep creases lined Shane's forehead. "It's hard to believe you knew nothing about the value—"

"Shane, wake up! All I knew was that my parents had bought a plot of land for their retirement. It was the only thing they'd ever owned. After Dad died, it was Mom's nest egg if she needed it. Mr. Gunthry says the price is up because a highway will run through the area."

"And you didn't know about that, either, right?"

She shook her head as tears came to her eyes. "You know, Shane, I used to think you were a kind, compassionate man who'd seen the worst part of life, but still tried to make it better for others. But with me, you're so hard and cold sometimes. It's ironic. You reunite people but you won't open your heart to reunite us. You don't trust me enough to let me get within ten yards, except when we make love and even then you hold back. Do you think I can't tell? Do you know how it hurts that you don't trust me enough to let me know all of you?"

He sat up and stared straight ahead. "Don't you know how it hurts me that I *can't* trust you?"

Hope's dreams withered. At the words that were so harsh now that they were out in the open, she knew what she had to say and what she had to do for all their sakes. "Shane, there's nothing I can do to prove I loved you then, and I love you now. You have to either believe me or not. That's up to you. I'm tired of trying to prove it. I'm tired of trying to earn your love, seek your approval, do and say the right thing so you don't distrust me more. Don't you think Christopher can feel the tension between us?"

"This afternoon won't happen again."

She stared at his profile, loving him but hurting too much to keep her feelings inside. "What will we do next time? Make sure the door's closed? A misunderstanding doesn't stay behind a closed door, neither does a lack of trust. The tension's not good for Christopher. It's not good for us. I can't live with you anymore, loving you but knowing you don't love me. I thought we could get back what we had, but I was wrong, so very wrong. We'll stay here through to-morrow, but then Christopher and I will go back to Aunt El's until I find a place of our own. I'll let you see Christopher whenever you want. You're his father, and I'll never interfere in your relationship with him."

Shane turned toward her then, his face hard, his jaw set until he said in a steel-edged voice, "If you leave, I'll sue for custody."

Hope didn't think the pain in her heart could get any worse, but she was wrong. "Do you want to trap me, Shane? Do you want to trap Christopher in an untenable situation? Don't you understand yet that love can't survive under those conditions? That's why I wouldn't trap you!''

His silence brought more tears to her eyes and sobs to her throat. She couldn't stand the coldness any longer. He was keeping all barriers in place, and she just didn't have the strength to knock them down, especially when she knew he wouldn't let her. She moved faster than she'd ever moved in her life. All she wanted to do was escape to her room so he couldn't see the extent of her devastation.

He gave no sign that he even saw her leave. She climbed the steps feeling as if Christmas would never come again.

The chill of the room didn't affect Shane as much as the chill around his heart. He felt cold inside. So cold, as though he'd never be warm again. He glanced at the steps. The hall light was out.

Dressing mechanically, he checked his pocket for his car keys, and then headed for the garage. There was someplace he had to go, someplace he went every holiday and many days in between. Except . . . he'd missed this Thanksgiving. He hadn't been there since Hope had arrived.

This late on Christmas Eve, there wasn't much traffic. Most people were home with their families. He turned into the cemetery with a sense of relief, a sense of the familiar. A few minutes later, he stood in front of the plaque with his son's name.

"Davie, how I wish you could talk to me. I wish you could let me feel you."

Silence. An absence of feeling. Numbness.

In trying to protect himself from getting hurt again, had he become numb to everything?

Yes.

"Davie?"

Shane felt emotion welling up inside him and didn't try to suffocate it. He let it rise, as uncomfortable and painful as it was. His heart raced, his chest tightened and he felt tears prick his eyes. Damn, it hurt. It hurt so much....

"Why did you leave, Davie? Why did my father leave, and my mom and Mary Beth? Why does everyone I love leave?"

The strength of the pain, the ache around Shane's heart, brought him to the ground. On his knees, he stared at his son's name and prayed for deliverance from the hurt, the loneliness, the emptiness. The chill of night swirled around him, the silence echoed his question over and over.

After a while, the echo stopped.

Hope is leaving, too.

"I knew she wouldn't stay."

You knew?

"She left before. She didn't love me enough...."

She loved you too much.

Too much.

Was it as simple as that? Had Hope's love been so pure and true she couldn't stand to see it compromised? And when she'd tried to love him again, he'd thrown it back in her face. No wonder she wanted to leave.

What had he done?

She'd said she couldn't stand to live with him knowing he didn't love her. But that wasn't true. He did love her. He'd loved her since he met her. But now it was too late. His father, mother, Davie and Mary Beth had left. He could do nothing to prevent their leaving. But Hope...

Tell her you love her.

Was that enough? What had she said—she couldn't prove to him that she loved him. But she had proved it, over and over again, with every act, every word, every touch. Could he undo the damage? Was trust simply a conscious decision?

No, it's a leap of faith.

"Davie, Davie, are you here?"

Silence answered Shane again, but a comforting sense of peace wound about him. He suddenly knew that he could do nothing about the past, but he was responsible for his future. Ungodly things happened, but that didn't mean there wasn't a God. Black wasn't always black, and white wasn't always white. Shades of both reflected the world in which he lived.

He felt shaken...different...changed. Changed in his heart and soul. But he was certain of one thing. He loved Hope, and love was something he couldn't turn his back on, not anymore. He needed her love, he'd just been too afraid to accept it. Now, somehow, he had to convince her that love was the wonderful gift she thought it was. He had to convince her he was worth another try.

As Shane rose to his feet, one star shined brighter than all the rest.

The garage door opening alerted Hope that Shane was leaving. She had no idea where he was going. Tears still lingered too near the surface for her to brush them away, for her to brush the hurt away. Had she really told Shane she was leaving? Wouldn't that be the best thing for everyone?

She uncurled her legs, pushed herself out of her bedroom chair and went to stand in the doorway to Christopher's room. He slept so peacefully, so innocently. Suddenly, she remembered his presents. She had to put them under the tree.

It took her three trips, and once she'd arranged them to her satisfaction, tears blurred her eyes all over again. Wrapping her arms around herself, she went to the kitchen to make a cup of tea. Through the kitchen window, she could see one star shining brighter than all the others. She opened the door and stepped out onto the porch.

With her hands on the balustrade, she gazed up at the bright white light. She loved Shane. As sure as the star was shining, she would never stop loving him.

So why are you leaving? The voice seemed to come from deep inside her.

"I can't keep battling his defenses. I can't keep trying to prove I love him."

Why not just love him?

The simplicity of the question stunned her. Was that the problem? That she was trying to prove something instead of just loving him? Could he sense that? Was she on guard, too?

She tried to remember what he'd said earlier. He'd said she'd called off the wedding. He'd sounded so hurt, so...abandoned. Shane had been abandoned over and over again. By his father, his mother, and in a way by his son and wife, too. Then Hope had left before their wedding. Did he expect the people he loved to leave him? Is that why he protected himself?

Of course. Why hadn't she seen it before?

Because she was as caught up in the present situation as he was. They'd been so busy guarding themselves, trying to make the marriage work....

If she left, she'd prove to him again that the people he loved deserted him.

But did he love her?

She thought about the birthday party he'd given her, his possessiveness, his support of her decision to go back to school, his passion and tenderness when he made love to her. He might not admit it, but he loved her. Shane wasn't a man to pretend anything.

So, what are you going to do?

She wouldn't leave. Like water on stone, she'd wear him down until he admitted what he felt. She'd do it by being herself and loving him. Tonight, her anger had gotten the best of her. Maybe tomorrow morning, in the light of day, he would listen to her. And if he didn't...

She heard the garage door open and close, and she held her breath.

* * *

First, Shane went up to Hope's room. This afternoon when the front door had slammed, he'd known she would be back. But tonight, with the quiet click of the guest-room door, he'd realized she'd never put her heart in his hands again. But maybe he could change that. Maybe...

When he found her room empty, he almost panicked. But with a quick look into Christopher's room and seeing his son sleeping, he knew she hadn't gone very far. Returning downstairs, he saw the dim glare of light from the kitchen. In his rush to see her, he'd missed it when he came in.

The back door stood open. With his heart thumping madly in his ears, he stepped outside. She was looking up at the sky, toward the brightest star, as if seeking guidance. He could use some of that himself.

"Hope?"

She turned, but her face was shadowed. He didn't know if she'd let him touch her, but he was beyond caring about logic or good sense. He took her hands in his. They were cold. He wanted to give her all the heat inside him, everything he could.

So he plunged in, praying she wouldn't shut him out the way he had her. Praying she'd listen. "I know you've made a decision, and you think it's for the best. But you're wrong." When her hands fluttered in his, he rushed on, "I've been an idiot. I was so afraid of letting myself love you, so afraid that you'd leave again, I've been driving you away. I don't have any excuse. I don't know what to say to make things right—"

"I've changed my mind about leaving," she interrupted in a quiet, gentle voice. "I love you, Shane. And someday you're going to wake up and see it. I'm going to talk to you about it, and touch you, and just simply love you until you let down some of those walls and let me in. If necessary, maybe we'll have to see a counselor..."

He saw the worried look on her face, the concern that he would argue with her, reject her again. But he saw the determination, too, and his heart swelled with even more love for her. "Everything you said today was true. I have been shutting you out. I don't want to do that ever again. Because I love you, Hope. And I don't want to lose you. I want you to help me see the shades between black and white and all the colors, too."

"You...love me?" She sounded breathless, as if she couldn't believe he was saying it.

"More than I ever thought possible. Since you and Christopher came into my life, I've felt the stirrings of happiness again." Looking deep into her eyes to make sure she understood, he went on, "I can trust you now because I've finally realized what a sacrifice you made four years ago. You put my needs before yours. Now I'm going to put your needs first for the rest of our lives. I didn't distrust *you*, Hope. I just didn't trust myself—to feel again, to love again. Can you forgive me? Can we start over?"

Tears ran down her cheeks. "I don't want to start over. I want to remember everything we've shared and go on from here."

He took her face between his palms and tenderly brushed the tears from her cheeks with his thumbs. "I've hurt you. I never meant to hurt you. I was so damn busy trying to protect myself...."

"Let's both forgive the hurt and concentrate on the love."

He encircled her with his arms and brought her closer. "I do love you, Hope. I'll spend every day for the rest of my life proving it."

"You don't have to prove anything. Just love me."

His lips found hers and made promises he knew he would keep for a lifetime. Hope promised back, lacing her hands in his hair, loving him.

Suddenly, a sound wound around them. Music? No. Chimes.

They both lifted their heads at the same time.

The chimes on the Christmas angel were moving gently against one another.

Hope's eyes rounded, then she smiled. "I guess Santa arrived."

Shane touched his finger to his tongue and held it up in the air. "Hope, there's no wind."

She laughed—a sound as sweet as the chimes. "No, there isn't. On Christmas Eve, there's magic . . . and miracles."

Shane pointed to the bright star. "That guided me home. And while it was guiding me—" he squeezed her closer "—I thought about what I'd say to you. I thought a lot about my life, about Davie and Christopher. About us. I realized what a gift children are. And I thought that maybe in a year or so, we could have another child, so Christopher can learn all about sharing firsthand."

"Shane, are you sure?" The question was a gasp of surprise.

He understood her astonishment; the idea had stunned him, as well. But he'd thought about it on the drive home. "Yes, I'm sure. And although Christopher needs a brother or sister, there's another more important reason I want to have another child—to show how much I love you."

Resting her hands on his shoulder, Hope said with certainty, "You can do that without us making a baby."

"I know. But I don't want any barriers, Hope. I want your heart to flow into mine and mine to flow into yours. I want it all."

She wound her arms around him and laid her cheek against his heart. "This truly is a night for miracles."

Shane held Hope tight against him and gazed at the star. A night for miracles . . . Christmas Eve, and he was so thankful he was holding his Christmas angel in his arms.

Epilogue

One year later

A bottle of champagne stood chilling on the nightstand beside the bed. Shane had fixed a tray of cheese and crackers while Hope showered. He'd bought a special present for her this Christmas, and he preferred giving it to her in their bed.

The bathroom door opened and Hope emerged, a white satin nightgown flowing with her as she came toward him. Shane swallowed hard. His pulse hammered, and as always when he saw her, his heart overflowed with love.

"You're breathtaking—my Christmas angel."

She arched her eyebrows. "I'm no angel and we both know it."

As she slid into the other side of the bed, he chuckled. "No, you're a lovely woman who's as stubborn as I am sometimes."

Smiling knowingly, she gestured to the food and champagne. "What's all this?"

"I thought we should celebrate. In my heart, Christmas Eve is really our anniversary. I guess I never told you everything that happened that night. We've been so happy, I didn't want to bring up anything to remind you of the rough times."

Hope sidled closer to him and laid her hand on his chest. "Don't you know by now you can tell me anything?"

Over the past year, he'd confided in her many times about his hopes and fears and dreams for their future. "I know. And I guess that's why I thought about this tonight. Why I want to tell you."

Curling beside him with her head on his shoulder, she urged, "So tell me."

He loved her there, beside him, always. "I told you I went to the cemetery last Christmas Eve and that the brightest star gave me hope and guided me back to you. What I didn't tell you was that I actually thought I heard a voice pointing my thinking in the right direction."

She popped up and looked into his eyes. "I did, too! When I was gazing at the star." She thought about it for a moment. "Do you think it was Davie, or for me—my mother?"

"Maybe. Or the same Christmas angel who touched the chimes. I don't know. But I do know I want to remember that night forever. I realized I had to let go of the past so I could believe in our love for the future. I thought you might want to remember it, too." He took a small box from between the pillows and set it in her lap. "Merry Christmas."

Her eyes glistened with tears.

"Don't cry yet. Open it first," he teased.

She tore off the bow and unwrapped the box. When she opened it, she gasped. A solitaire diamond surrounded by smaller ones twinkled up at her. "The star!"

She'd guessed without him telling her. "Do you like it?"

"It's beautiful. Will you put it on for me?"

He took the ring from the box and slid it onto her finger above the wedding band. "The jeweler said women wear rings like that with their bands. But if you think it's too much, you can wear it on your other hand."

She leaned over and gave him a kiss that told him it wasn't too much, it was just right. When he drew her on top of him so he could show her how much he loved her, she resisted and leaned away.

"What's wrong?"

She smiled and smoothed her hand over his forehead. "Nothing. Except I want to give you your gift, too. It's just not quite as tangible...yet."

"I don't understand."

"Well, I can munch on the cheese and crackers, but I can't have any champagne."

He saw the glow on her face, the new lushness to her body he thought came from being happily married, and he knew. "You're pregnant!"

She nodded. "The doctor confirmed it this morning. Are you...pleased?"

They'd talked about having another child many times, but had decided to let it happen naturally without giving the matter undue attention. "Yes, I'm pleased. But what about your degree? I know how much you want to teach...."

"I'll be finished with most of the coursework before the baby's born. And as far as teaching...I'll watch *our* children grow and then I'll teach."

"You teach Christopher every day. And you've taught me everything I know about love." He kissed her, and this time when he drew her on top of him, she didn't resist.

He broke the kiss only to murmur, "Merry Christmas, Mrs. Walker."

Tracing her fingers over his lips, she smiled. "Merry Christmas, Mr. Walker."

Shane reached to the nightstand and switched off the light.

But the room still glowed with their love. As Shane told Hope again with words and kisses and touches how much he loved her, one brilliant star twinkled at them through the window. In the distance, chimes played delicately, yet no wind blew.

Because it was Christmas Eve—a night for love, magic and miracles.

*   *   *   *   *

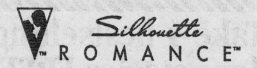

COMING NEXT MONTH

#1132 SHEIK DADDY—Barbara McMahon
Super Fabulous Fathers
Years ago, Sheik "Ben" Shalik had loved Megan O'Sullivan with his whole heart. Now he was back, ready to sweep her off her feet. But could he forgive Megan for keeping their daughter a secret?

#1133 MAIL ORDER WIFE—Phyllis Halldorson
Valentine Brides
Mail order bride Coralie Dixon expected anything from her husband-to-be, except outright rejection! Handsome bachelor Jim Buckley *said* he wasn't interested, but his actions spoke differently....

#1134 CINDERELLA BRIDE—Christine Scott
Valentine Brides
Tall, dark and stirringly handsome, Ryan Kendrick was a perfect Prince Charming. But his "convenient" wedding proposal was hardly the fairy-tale marriage Cynthia Gilbert had been hoping for!

#1135 THE HUSBAND HUNT—Linda Lewis
Valentine Brides
Sarah Brannan was all set to say "I do." But then Jake Logan asked her to *live* with him—not marry him. So Sarah set out to turn the reluctant Jake into her willing groom.

#1136 MAKE-BELIEVE MOM—Elizabeth Sites
Valentine Brides
Prim and proper Laura Gardiner was shocked by rancher Nick Rafland's scandalous proposal. Nick needed a make-believe mom for his little nieces, not a real wife. But Laura wanted to be a true-blue bride....

#1137 GOING TO THE CHAPEL—Alice Sharpe
Valentine Brides
Elinor Bosley ran a wedding chapel, though she'd vowed never to walk down its aisle. Then she met sexy Tom Rex and his adorable four-year-old son. And Elinor started hearing wedding bells of her own!

Take 4 bestselling love stories FREE
Plus get a FREE surprise gift!

Bestselling author

RACHEL LEE

takes her Conard County series to new heights with

A CONARD COUNTY Reckoning

This March, Rachel Lee brings readers a brand-new,
longer-length, out-of-series title featuring the characters
from her successful Conard County miniseries.

Janet Tate and Abel Pierce have both been betrayed and
carry deep, bitter memories. Brought together by great
passion, they must learn to trust again.

"Conard County is a wonderful place to visit! Rachel Lee
has crafted warm, enchanting stories. These are wonderful
books to curl up with and read. I highly recommend them."
—*New York Times* bestselling author
Heather Graham Pozzessere

Available in March, wherever Silhouette books are sold.

INTRODUCING...  WINNER'S CIRCLE

A collection of award-winning books by award-winning
authors! From Harlequin and Silhouette.

VALENTINE'S NIGHT
by Penny Jordan

VOTED BESTSELLING
HARLEQUIN PRESENTS!

Let award-winning Penny Jordan bring you a Valentine you
won't forget. *Valentine's Night* is full of sparks as our heroine
finds herself snowed in, stranded and sharing a bed with an
attractive stranger who makes thoughts of her fiancé fly
out the window.

"Women everywhere will find pieces of themselves in Jordan's
characters."   —*Publishers Weekly*

Available this February wherever Harlequin books are sold.

WC-2

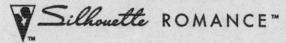

Cupid is on the loose...so bachelors beware, 'cause here come the

VALENTINE BRIDES

This February, Silhouette Romance invites you to spend the most romantic holiday of the year celebrating the joys of wedded bliss. Whether it's convincing that reluctant groom to say "I do" or advertising for a wife and mother—these special stories about love and marriage are the perfect Valentine's Day treat!

Don't miss:

When Cupid strikes, marriage is sure to follow! Don't miss the weddings—this February, only from

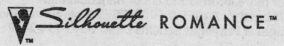

Silhouette ROMANCE™

VALBRIDE

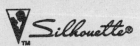